Ellie
and the
Underworld

A novel by

S. L. Saunders

FIRST EDITION
Published in 2023 by
GREEN CAT BOOKS
19 St Christopher's Way
Pride Park
Derby
DE24 8JY

www.green-cat.shop

ISBN: 978-1-913794-49-1

DEDICATION

My dedication goes to my lovely children,
who have always held onto hope.

CONTENTS

1

Have you ever experienced one of those days—a dreary, chilly day with nothing eventful happening? This was the type of day Ellie McKay was having as she walked home from school in the rain, thinking of happier times. Her boots squelched through the puddles as the rain soaked her clothes, and she couldn't wait to be home in the warmth. As she approached the end of the lane in Stony Brook village, her spirits lifted a little as she caught sight of the cottage she shared with her dad.

Ellie quickened her pace, eager to escape inside. As she entered the property, she made herself a mug of hot chocolate, kicked off her shoes, and flopped onto the red velour couch. Letting out an enormous sigh of relief, she was grateful to be back in her cosy home.

She hugged the cushion for comfort, imagining the faint scent of her mum's perfume. At 15 years old, she struggled with depression, and the memories of her mum only intensified those feelings.

Ellie longed for an adventure to break the monotony of her bleak reality. She yawned, feeling the weight of tiredness settling in. Sitting on the couch, she listened to the icy rain on the window. Her hands wrapped around the mug of hot chocolate, instantly warming her cold fingertips.

After finishing her drink, she snuggled up and waited for her dad to come home from work. She closed her eyes to let sleep take over her tired body. However, her plan was abruptly interrupted when a piece of ice hit the window. 'Bang!' Another chunk of ice hit the window, which caused Ellie to jump up and see an orb the size of a watermelon hovering outside, pushing its way through the glass.

Ellie's heart raced as she watched the orb glow within an orange flame as it pushed through the window and hovered in the air. Rooted to the spot, she struggled to comprehend what had just happened. The pulsating orb observed her as if it had a mind of its own. She rubbed her eyes and pinched herself, questioning whether she was hallucinating, but the orb remained, defying the laws of gravity and logic.

She took a step closer to the orb, and it moved in response, its flames dancing in a hypnotic rhythm. Ellie was both terrified and mesmerised, wondering what had just presented itself. A loud noise generated from the orb, causing Ellie's ears to ring. She watched in horror as the orb shattered into several icy shards. Quickly, she dropped to the ground and curled up in a ball to avoid being hit by any of the flying fragments.

When she opened her eyes, the orb was gone, and a young man appeared in its place. He stood tall, brushing off his vibrant yellow suit. The purple chiffon cravat and shiny white shoes completed his outfit. Ellie couldn't help but think he looked dressed to impress. She gaped at him in disbelief, wondering if she was dreaming.

"What...what just happened?" Ellie stammered, trying to make sense of it.

The young man grinned, clearly pleased with himself. "Wow, that worked!" he exclaimed. "That is the first time I have changed solid atoms in glass to a non-frozen state. I worked on how to quickly change the molecular structure of amorphous solids like glass, and it allowed me to polymorph through your window."

Ellie found it hard to understand what the young man was saying but was also distracted by the window's peculiar behaviour. The bulge in the glass she'd noticed earlier had slowly reduced in size until it vanished completely as if nothing had occurred.

"I suppose I could have entered your home conventionally, but where would the fun be in that."

Ellie still couldn't make sense of his words and found herself staring at him in confusion. "Who are you?"

"Hello, Octavian is the name. Nice to be in your company."

The young man extended his hand towards Ellie, and after hesitating, she eventually returned the gesture. Her eyes widened in shock as she felt a strange suction feeling. When she pulled her hand away, she realised that he wasn't entirely human.

Ellie observed that the young Octavian possessed an unusually large head with enormous, dark eyes. His complexion was grey with a bluish hue, and he was a frail figure standing over six feet tall.

Shocked, she struggled to speak and kept a safe distance from him, her voice trembling. "What are you, and how did you get in here?" Ellie asked, trying to understand how Octavian had managed to get through the window. "I'm sorry if I sound rude, but it doesn't make any sense. How is that even possible?"

Octavian spoke slowly and gently. "I understand it must be a lot to take in," he acknowledged. "I used quantum transportation to move through the window, and I was sent to you by an organisation called the 'Underworld', to act as your guardian."

Ellie still couldn't believe what she was hearing and scowled at Octavian in disbelief.

"And why do I need a guardian? I have my dad to look after me," she added, feeling defensive.

Octavian looked at her, his expression unreadable. "You should sit down; you've gone pale and look like you have seen a ghost." Octavian's words brought her back to the present moment.

"You're right, I feel a bit lightheaded," Ellie admitted and sat down on the couch, trying to take it all in.

Octavian rummaged in his pocket and pulled out a shiny amulet. It was hung on a silver chain, and he held it towards her.

"Your mother left this in the Underworld, with instructions for it to be delivered to you when the time was right."

Ellie's eyes narrowed, and a spark of anger flashed in them. Six years had passed since her mum had died, and the grief still weighed heavily on her.

She had many questions she needed to ask. "How did you find me?"

Octavian hesitated and shuffled around. "The Underworld has its ways," he said cryptically. "But that's not important now, your safety is!"

Ellie shook her head in disbelief. "This is insane," she muttered. "How can you expect me to believe all this?"

"Your mum was an amazing woman with extraordinary powers. You will learn this in time. My instructions are to give you the amulet and for you to never take it off." Ellie listened, her mind racing about what her mum's powers were and the nature of the Underworld's agenda.

She stood with her shoulders hunched, wanting to move away as Octavian moved behind her and secured the amulet around her neck. He fumbled clumsily to close the clasp with his tentacle-like fingers. Ellie shuddered at his touch; his hands were icy cold.

"Thank you."

Although still panic-stricken, she didn't feel as fearful of Octavian as when he had first appeared.

She examined the amulet. It was a silver oval shape with a grey-marbled stone in the centre, and she noticed an inscription engraved around it that read, 'ABRACADABRA'. Ellie couldn't help but laugh, which caused Octavian to look confused.

"Is this amusing?" he asked.

She apologised for her laughter. "Is it meant to protect me?" she enquired. "I'm just used to hearing 'abracadabra' at birthday parties when magicians pull rabbits out of hats."

Octavian acknowledged her amusement with a chuckle before replying, "That old chestnut. I understand. But don't underestimate the power of the word 'abracadabra'. It has an ancient magical meaning. Wearing the amulet can keep you safe, ward off evil, and even help you create magic if you need it." Her mind swirled with confusion; it was as if she had been transported to a fantasy world.

She watched as Octavian started to perspire. "I feel faint," he expressed, wiping his forehead. "It's very warm in here. It's not good for me; I could lose too much salt and become unwell."

Ellie observed droplets of sweat trickling down his larger-than-average forehead.

"Please, could I have a glass of water with a teaspoon of salt in it? I need to drink, or I will dehydrate. I know this sounds odd and I would never recommend drinking salt water as it would make you very sick, but my circumstances are very unique," Octavian pleaded. Ellie quickly assessed the situation and rushed to the kitchen to get a glass of saltwater.

What if Octavian died? How would she explain his death to her dad, or anyone for that matter? She filled the glass with water, added the salt, and rushed back to him. As soon as Octavian drank the salt water, he visibly improved.

"It's time for me to go. Your dad will be back soon. I can't risk bumping into him just yet," Octavian declared.

Ellie nodded, feeling relieved that he was leaving. "I agree," she said. "This isn't an ideal situation for my dad to come home to."

"Can you meet me at the old oak tree next to the church at one in the afternoon tomorrow?" Octavian asked.

The oak tree was Ellie's favourite spot, and she often sought solace under its branches after school. Being close to nature and feeling the earth beneath her feet always helped ground her. Ellie didn't trust Octavian and was aware of the danger of meeting strangers. She also didn't like lying to her dad. She pondered what to do and then had an idea.

"I could leave a note for my dad, telling him I've gone out with friends from school."

"I understand your concern, Ellie, and I don't wish to cause you any harm."

She remembered her dad had installed a tracker and safety alarm on her phone after her mum's death.

If anything were to happen, her dad would be able to locate her.

"Yes, I'll come and meet you," Ellie answered.

"This is wonderful news, I will leave by the back door this time, much easier than turning back into an orb. Farewell, and see you tomorrow." No sooner than he had appeared in her front room, the strange Octavian had now departed.

Ellie still wasn't sure if the last hour had been a dream or reality, but the empty glass with salt residue was proof of what had happened. Exhausted, she slumped back down on the couch. The amulet around her neck pulsated and glowed purple, she was sure it had been a silver colour earlier. Ellie didn't have time to dwell on the situation as her dad would be home soon.

It was a Friday, and her dad had spent the entire day working on the farm with Grandpa Jo. He was due back around five o'clock. Ellie had always preferred to be there when he came home from work. It helped to lessen the silence in the house since 'that dreadful day'.

As soon as Bill got home, he entered the front room to greet her. "It's been a tough day at work today," he grumbled. "I've been chasing after sheep. Some kids camping left the gate open again."

Bill was a sturdy man with a ruddy complexion and tousled dark hair. Some would call him a handsome man but that was of no concern to him, he still loved his wife.

Ellie couldn't help but notice the sweat on his forehead and the exhaustion in his eyes. She placed a cup of steaming tea in front of him and offered a warm smile, feeling relieved that her dad was too preoccupied to see her flustered state.

She knew that her dad had been working at Pear Tree Farm since he was 20 years old. Now, two decades later, he still assisted Grandpa Jo, who at 66, required all the help he could get. During the week, he worked part-time as an accountant for a multinational electric company, earning a decent enough salary to pay the bills. As a widowed parent, he needed a good income. Ellie knew her dad loved the farm, and the accounting job was merely a means to an end.

She watched as her dad smiled at her. "So, how was your day, Ellie?"

She brushed her long, dark hair over her shoulder and forced a smile. She had always been self-conscious about her appearance, despite her pretty features: freckled skin, petite lips, and blue eyes that sparkled against her pale complexion. Ellie's cheeks flushed, knowing she was about to lie to her dad. She had never felt comfortable lying, but today she had no choice.

Ellie fidgeted with her fingers as she spoke, trying to keep her voice steady. "The same old thing, nothing eventful." She placed the amulet on the table. "But I did find something interesting by the oak tree. It is an amulet; it was buried in the soil. I cleaned it up, and it looks like new."

Ellie observed a shift in her dad's demeanour and tone as he glanced at the amulet.

"Where did you say you found it? It looks familiar," he asked, appearing on edge. Ellie's stomach churned with guilt.

"I found it by the oak tree," she responded, her voice becoming more hesitant.

"You need to be careful picking up things that are not yours. You don't know who it belonged to or who might come looking for it," Bill cautioned as he pushed his plate aside. Ellie sensed her dad's unease and enquired, "Are you alright?"

"No, I'm not, I am going to bed. I don't appear to have too much of an appetite. It's been a tough day with all the sheep running me ragged. We will talk tomorrow. Love you."

Ellie watched as her dad walked up the stairs, his body slumping heavily.

"Love you too," she called after him.

She felt concerned, as her dad was usually in good spirits despite their struggles. But tonight, something was different. Ellie suspected he was troubled by more than just fatigue, he looked anxious as if the weight of the world was on his shoulders. She made her way to bed and hoped a good sleep would help.

The early morning crow of the cockerel awoke Ellie, and she groaned and tried to go back to sleep, covering her head with her pillow. A few moments later, she heard the front door shut. This was unusual because her dad always said goodbye before leaving. Getting out of bed, she peered out of her window to catch a glimpse of him driving down the lane. Anxiety fluttered inside of her; something was wrong.

Ellie had planned to meet Octavian at one o'clock, but she was still uncertain whether yesterday's encounter with him had been real or just a dream. The amulet hanging around her neck suddenly pulsed, confirming the events of yesterday.

Setting her plans in motion for the day, she took a shower and had breakfast. With a satisfied stomach, Ellie made her way to her bedroom to get dressed. She opted for her favourite pink jumper, a pair of well-worn jeans, and comfortable walking boots. As she looked out the window, she observed the remains of some frost on the ground but took note of the clear blue sky and decided against bringing a coat. The weather was perfect for her meeting with Octavian.

Ellie took a deep breath, trying to steady herself as she walked towards the church in the distance. Each step took her further away from safety, and her nerves were frayed. Her heart pounded in her chest as she listened to the rustle of the leaves and the chirping of the birds, each sound growing louder with every passing moment. She couldn't shake the feeling of impending doom. Despite it all, she kept moving forward, determined to meet Octavian no matter what.

Ellie's eyes darted around the area, hoping to catch a glimpse of him. But he was nowhere to be seen. A wave of uncertainty washed over her, making her question her sanity. She approached the old oak tree and leaned against its knobbly trunk, seeking solace in its familiar presence; little did she know that her life was about to take a drastic turn.

The beautiful blue sky that had been present, quickly turned black as the thunder boomed through the air. Ellie's body jolted in fright. She looked up and saw the lightning bolts striking the ground, illuminating everything with a blinding light. Despite knowing that hiding under the old oak tree during a storm was risky, she had nowhere else to go. Ellie weighed her options carefully, but another deafening boom of thunder shook the ground, pushing her to make a quick decision.

With her heart racing, she decided to run to the nearby church for shelter. However, before she could even move, a bolt of lightning struck the tree with intense force. The impact threw Ellie backwards, causing her to hit her head on the ground; her vision was momentarily blurred, and she felt disorientated.

As Ellie regained her senses, she realised something had changed. She wasn't outside anymore. Looking around, she found herself in a dark, hollow cylinder with a floor beneath her. The place was unfamiliar, and panic started to rise within her, and she could feel her heart beating faster and faster. She stifled a scream and realised she was trapped inside the trunk of the old oak tree.

Ellie began to explore the inside of the tree trunk and her fingers brushed against its rough surface until she felt a switch. Without hesitation, she flipped it up, and a soft glow illuminated the space, revealing a toboggan with steps leading down to it. She paused for a moment, unsure of what to do next, but curiosity got the better of her, and she climbed inside the toboggan.

The seat was positioned vertically, with the downward slope beckoning her towards the unknown. As she settled into the seat, she spotted a button marked 'exit.' Not taking any chances, she pulled the harness over herself and it clicked into place like a rollercoaster restraint. Taking a deep breath, Ellie pressed the red exit button, and the toboggan sprang to life.

The sudden flash of lights and blaring siren caught her off guard, as she hurtled down the tree at breakneck speed. Her heart pounded in her chest as she clutched the harness, grateful for its secure hold. After what felt like an eternity, the toboggan came to an abrupt stop, leaving Ellie breathless and shaken. Taking a moment to collect herself, she unclasped the harness and stepped out of the toboggan. Looking around, Ellie took in her new surroundings, feeling a mix of excitement and apprehension.

She heard a voice behind her and turned to see Octavian, a wide smile on his face.

"Greetings, Miss Ellie. Did you enjoy your journey?" he asked as he placed an arm around her shoulder.

She couldn't help but feel relieved to see a familiar face, especially after the harrowing ride.

"It was dramatic and stressful," Ellie replied, still trying to catch her breath.

Octavian chuckled, unfazed by her response. "You will find it easier the next time. The first ride is always the scariest," he reassured her. "We call them Boggopods, our new advanced way to travel to the Underworld. An improvement on the old way, they are environmentally friendly and run from bioenergy sources."

Ellie couldn't help but smile at his enthusiasm for the new mode of transportation. It was clear Octavian felt proud of the innovation and excited to share it with her. She was grateful for his company and felt a sense of relief that she was not alone in this unfamiliar place.

Her eyes widened at Octavian's unique attire, a green suit composed of tiny leaves and a matching velvet top hat. She couldn't help but admire his bold fashion sense, but her curiosity about her current whereabouts overshadowed her thoughts.

"Octavian, can you tell me where we are now?" she asked, hoping for an answer.

"No time for that now, Miss Ellie. We mustn't be late for the Grand Council meeting. Bob doesn't take kindly to tardiness. Please follow me," Octavian answered with a sense of urgency in his voice, as he began to move quickly.

Ellie hesitated for a moment, unsure if she should follow, but the thought of being lost and alone in an unknown place outweighed her reservations. She hastened her steps to keep up with Octavian's wobbly and fast-paced gait, determined not to lose sight of him.

2

Ellie watched as Octavian straightened his suit, using his tentacle fingers to carefully adjust the leaves.

"Octavian, your outfit is impressive."

He smiled at her and shook his head in amusement. "You, on the other hand, look like you've been dragged through a bush backwards," Octavian quipped, causing her to let out a loud laugh at the unexpected comment.

She looked up at Octavian, hoping he had a solution to tame her wild hair. "I don't suppose you have a hairbrush in that fancy suit of yours?" she asked, gesturing towards his green outfit.

Octavian's brow furrowed slightly as he tipped his top hat forward, revealing a bald head.

"Ellie, I do not need a hairbrush. I lost mine at a young age," he replied with a sigh.

Ellie felt a pang of guilt for her assumption and quickly apologised. "I'm so sorry, I didn't know." She opted to flatten her hair down with her hand, hoping it would at least look presentable.

As she followed Octavian down the narrow, dimly lit corridor, she felt the dampness in the air and noticed tree branches that entwined in the walls, with brightly coloured, unusual bugs crawling on them. The bugs whispered to each other, creating an eerie atmosphere.

As they approached a wooden door with a cast iron doorknocker, Octavian turned to Ellie with a concerned look on his face. She couldn't help but wonder what was behind the door but decided not to ask.

"I want to remind you, Ellie, that this situation may be intense. I expressed my concern to the Grand Council before we arrived." She could sense the apprehension in Octavian's voice and smiled, determined not to let her nerves get the better of her.

"Thank you for looking out for me, Octavian. I can handle it," she replied confidently.

Octavian knocked three times on the door, and a voice demanded the password. Ellie watched as he searched his memory, trying to recall it.

After a moment, his face lit up with recognition. "Ah, yes, the password is 'Starlight'."

Ellie strained her eyes to glimpse who was behind the door as it slowly creaked open. She caught sight of a small turquoise creature with legs, arms, and giant orange eyes with huge black pupils. The creature reminded her of an upright hedgehog, but with a strange round belly and standing only two feet tall.

"Afternoon, Mr Octavian Dibble and Miss Ellie," the little creature greeted them, its voice high-pitched and cheerful.

Octavian returned the greeting, "Afternoon and good day to you too, Oggle Boggle." Ellie mused at the little creature's name and appearance.

"Please enter; the meeting is just about to start."

The door opened fully, and Ellie's eyes widened as she took in the sight before her. Behind the door was a large circular-shaped room, with several tiers and seating sections. Each area housed diverse animals, insects, creatures, and what resembled humans.

Ellie could see a giant snail next to a humanoid figure with green skin, sitting together in one section. In another section, a group of brightly coloured birds perched on a branch-like structure. Octavian gently nudged her forward, and she followed, trying not to stare too much.

Ellie clung to Octavian's arm, feeling overwhelmed. As they made their way towards their seats, a heated debate involving several polar bears caught her attention, in a section made from ice. She couldn't help but gasp at the sight, feeling both intimidated and fascinated. A loud growl emanated from one of them.

"The polar caps cannot melt anymore; we are losing our homes and sources of food. Where will we live? What will we eat? Many of my family must switch to eating plant vegetation. We are facing extinction, so many of us are gone already; I blame the humans." As he spoke, he glanced at Ellie, who quickly turned away in fear.

Ellie felt relieved when Octavian led her to a section on the lowest tier, where she saw other humans. They greeted her politely, but she still felt out of place amidst the diverse creatures and animals surrounding her. She observed Octavian wobbling off to an area with a pool, and to her surprise, he transformed into a fully formed octopus once in the water. She watched in amazement as he swam around effortlessly.

The sound of the gavel hitting the table caused a loud noise that echoed through the room.

A gruff voice broke the silence. "Humans, humans, humans! What can we do about them? Grrr."

Ellie gulped anxiously and wondered if the speaker saw her as an enemy. He took a deep breath and appeared to calm down. Ellie listened as his tone softened.

"However, we need them to work with us to save our planet, or many of us will become extinct. It pains me to say we need their help."

As he spoke, she noticed a wave of emotions sweep across the room. Some creatures appeared sad, and others looked angry. It was clear that the topic of working with humans was a contentious issue among the species in the Underworld.

The speaker was Mr Bob Bomtane, a badger, and the current head of the Grand Council. He had personally invited Ellie to attend. Mr Bomtane was fiercely loyal to the Underworld's survival and protective of his family, including his three cubs. She observed his long, sharp claws and how his bulky size added to his intimidating presence and couldn't help but feel a sense of awe and fear. As he walked around the table, Mr Bomtane made his way towards the human area and sniffed, curling his claws around his snout.

"Ah, Ellie, you have attended today; this is good." Ellie nodded in agreement, grateful for the warm welcome. She noticed that his demeanour softened as he spoke to her, and his defensive posture relaxed.

"We must arrange a personal meeting together soon," Bob continued, before turning his attention back to the rest of the room. "Thank you all for attending. We will not have a full meeting today. Young Ellie needs a lesson from Mr Octavian Dibble. Until that has taken place, I find it inappropriate to discuss delicate matters out of respect for our new visitor." Ellie observed the creatures in the room as they nodded in agreement and the sound of their unified response echoed across the different sections.

The room came to life with a flurry of movement and noise as the various species went about their business. Ellie looked around and a young male caught her eye as he gave her a friendly smile. He extended his hand towards her in greeting.

"Hi, I'm Kyle. I can show you around this place if you would like?"

She examined him carefully, noting his human-like appearance, with mousy-coloured hair and tanned skin. He wore baggy jeans and an oversized, well-worn black jumper.

"Okay, you can show me around. That would be nice. I feel like I'm in a completely different world," Ellie confided, with a hint of relief in her voice. She followed Kyle as they walked towards a section of the room with a large greenhouse.

As they approached the greenhouse, Ellie opened the door and a wave of heat hit her face, making her squint. Kyle instructed her to close the door.

"Just look through the glass; it helps to keep their ecosystem pure and uncontaminated."

As she peered through the glass she saw plants, reptiles, and insects all cohabitating happily in their shared environment. Kyle excitedly grabbed Ellie's arm as he pushed his way towards a small path.

"If we stay on this path, we will find King Jamari of the Sumatran tigers."

"So, what can you tell me about the King?" Ellie curiously asked.

"The King is graceful, cunning, and an excellent strategist when it comes to fighting. We need for him to remain an ally of the Underworld." Ellie nodded, taking in the information as they walked down the path.

As they turned the corner, she gazed in awe at the sight of an impressive tiger seated on a bamboo throne in the jungle area. His fur was thick and luxurious, and she couldn't resist the urge to run her fingers through it, but she knew not to attempt such a thing. The King sprung up from his throne and landed on his big paws. Ellie was unsure whether he had wanted to intimidate her, or if she just felt scared of being so close to this magnificent animal.

King Jamari fixed his gaze on Kyle and Ellie.

"Kyle, what brings you and our new visitor to my domain? My time is valuable, so quickly make your request."

Kyle cleared his throat before speaking. "Your Highness, we were hoping for your guidance and expertise in the current situation. You are aware we are facing the potential of a new rebellion, from Katia. We seek your wisdom to help us find a peaceful solution." Ellie watched as the King's expression darkened.

"I have been considering joining Katia and the rebellion," he said, his voice low and menacing. "My loyalty lies with my fellow animals. I will not stand by and watch as they suffer at the hands of humans." Jamari growled and fixed his gaze on Ellie as he circled her.

"I sense your fear." Ellie didn't dare move.

"It's alright, Ellie. I will not harm you, and I know you will not harm me." He brushed against her legs, making them shake and feel like jelly.

"King Jamari, please reconsider waging war against the humans. It will only lead to bloodshed. They will come armed with guns and shoot you," Kyle pleaded.

The King's mood shifted quickly; he reared up in the air and growled ferociously, then dropped back on all fours, extending his sharp claws as a display of his strength and power.

He let out a deep growl, causing Ellie to flinch. "I have heard such promises before, but nothing has changed. I will not sit idly by while my kind fades into extinction."

With a heavy heart, Kyle spoke up. "We understand your position, King Jamari. We will leave you to your thoughts." The King nodded curtly and disappeared into the dense jungle.

Ellie was caught off guard as Octavian appeared behind her.

"Tough meeting with the King, huh?" Ellie nodded, and Octavian put a comforting arm around her.

He led her past a pen containing a mix of sheep, cows, rats, and pigs. She noticed there was something different about them, they were too quiet and barely moving.

"Octavian, what's wrong with these animals?" Ellie asked, gesturing to the group of odd-looking creatures in the pen. "Why are they so still and quiet?"

"Unfortunately, these are the cloned animals; they were rescued after some humans, who claimed to be scientists, experimented on them. They lost their freedom and rights when the scientists took away their choice to live freely. The ones we rescued are now in our rehabilitation programme. We hope it works, so they can regain some normalcy," Octavian explained, leading Ellie away from the pen.

Ellie and Octavian turned the corner and entered a door that led to a tunnelled corridor. The walls were made of toughened glass, and the space resembled an aquarium, the kind you would visit on a family day out. Soft ambient music filled the air, and fluorescent lighting illuminated the way.

Ellie marvelled at the vast array of marine life swimming behind the glass. She saw shoals of brightly coloured fish, graceful sea turtles, and even a majestic manta ray gliding effortlessly through the water. The sight was mesmerising and gave her the sense of being at peace.

Octavian placed his hand on the glass as he explained the sight before them.

"You know, this is part of the ocean that you can see and not some artificial tank filled with water. It houses all our marine friends, large and small." Ellie felt a sense of joy as she watched the beauty of the ocean before her.

"That's so cool. I have never been one to support the entrapment of marine life. I find it cruel," Ellie expressed. Octavian nodded in agreement.

"Shall we eat?" Octavian suggested. Her stomach grumbled at the mention of food, and she eagerly followed him to the dining room.

The room was spacious and inviting, with open fires burning in the corners and fresh lavender incense filling the air. As they walked, Ellie noticed various doors and corridors leading off to other areas, each designed to evoke a sense of peace and tranquillity.

Octavian rang a small bell on the table and within seconds a young girl appeared. She was holding two oval plates, each adorned with a colourful arrangement of flowers. Ellie found it peculiar, and she wondered how a plate of flowers could satisfy her hunger. The girl handed her one of the plates.

"Hi, I'm Amber." The young girl greeted Ellie with a warm smile.

"Hello," Ellie replied, feeling a little awkward. She watched as the young girl cleared the tables around them and realised they were of a similar age. Amber caught her watching and continued to politely address Ellie.

"See you later, have a great time with Octi." Amber smiled as she walked away, her emerald eyes twinkling, adding to her beauty. Ellie admired Amber's stunning waist-length red hair that complemented her dark skin.

Octavian noticed the confusion on Ellie's face as she examined the plate of food in front of her. She longed for a bowl of her dad's homemade tomato soup with warm, freshly baked bread, but she didn't want to appear impolite by complaining.

Octavian offered her some guidance. "Ellie, think of your favourite food and take a forkful of the flowers, but be cautious, if you're not attentive you may end up with a horrible taste in your mouth," he warned her.

Ellie followed his advice and took a mouthful of the flowers. To her surprise, she could taste warm tomato soup, along with the hot, buttery bread. She looked at Octavian in wonder.

"Oh, my goodness, this is incredible! Who came up with this concept?"

Octavian's joy was evident as he explained the secret behind the magical-tasting flowers. "Our chef at the Underworld is a culinary mastermind. He takes pride in creating weekly signature dishes. Of course, not all of them are successful, but it is always fun trying them. We never know what to expect."

Ellie listened intently. "That's amazing!" she exclaimed. "I never would have thought to try flowers in my food."

Octavian chuckled. "Go ahead and think of another food, each mouthful brings a new taste sensation, I promise."

Ellie closed her eyes and imagined a knickerbocker glory, her favourite dessert. As she took a bite of the flower, she was rewarded with the taste of ice cream, complete with the cherry on top. Octavian waited as Ellie savoured the experience before announcing it was time for her first lesson.

3

Ellie watched as Octavian strode towards the wall and seized the interactive whiteboard, his spindly fingers tapping it swiftly. The board lit up, displaying a document with the words 'World Conservation Union.' A list of categories followed:

Endangered Species.
Critically Endangered Species.
Vulnerable Species.

As she read through the lists, her heart sank at the sight of the 'Sumatran tiger' under the critically endangered group and the polar bear under the vulnerable list. The number of endangered species seemed endless, and the reasons for their endangerment were equally disheartening: global warming, environmental pollution, deforestation, and poaching.

"I don't understand, how can I help the Underworld?" she questioned, her voice laced with uncertainty.

"We need your help for several reasons. Let me show you why." He walked over to the wall and pulled down a large map of the world. "You see, the Underworld has agents all over the world, working to protect it from threats. But we can't do it alone. We need someone with your unique abilities."

Ellie looked at him, confused. "Which abilities?"

Octavian turned back to her. "Ellie, you are an elemental. A fire elemental, to be precise. This means you have natural abilities that can be valuable to us. With the right training, you can learn to harness these powers and use them for good."

Ellie's eyes widened in shock. "What are you talking about? I don't have any powers."

Octavian smiled. "You'll see. Just give it a chance. With your abilities, you can start fires with your mind, cause volcanoes to erupt, and even create thunderbolt lightning storms."

Ellie listened in horror as Octavian continued to explain the extent of her powers.

"This is insane," she muttered to herself. "This is too much to take in. I want to go home, please."

"Ellie, we are trying not to overload you, as teaching you will be more appropriate. There are four of us, including yourself, and we represent all the elements. By ourselves, we are weaker, but together as four, we are a force to be reckoned with. The Underworld will need us to unite to bring balance to the planet," Octavian explained. Ellie felt her mind spinning, and she grew dizzy, and everything went black.

"Ellie, Ellie."

As her consciousness returned, she heard a gentle voice calling her name. Blinking her eyes, she opened them and saw the familiar faces of Kyle and Amber leaning over her. Octavian hurriedly approached with a glass of water. Ellie sat up slowly and took a sip of the water, feeling its coolness soothe her parched throat. Amber sat beside her, holding her hand tightly, providing comfort and reassurance.

"You are not by yourself in this, all of us are different elementals," Kyle said, standing tall with pride. "I represent air," he continued, gesturing to himself, "and Octavian is water," he added, nodding towards Octavian.

"And I represent earth," Amber chimed in, giving Ellie a reassuring smile.

Ellie listened as Kyle began to explain his abilities.

"I can start hurricanes, tornadoes, and ferocious winds." She couldn't help but feel overwhelmed by the power possessed by the elementals.

Ellie observed with appreciation as Octavian began to explain his powers.

"I can flood areas of land, freeze water, and I can swim underwater with no need for oxygen." Ellie looked on in bewilderment.

"It was not always like this," Octavian explained, his voice exuding enthusiasm. "In time, you can learn from Kyle and Amber how they got their gifts. As for me, mine came about under traumatic circumstances." Ellie looked at her three newfound associates with concern, nodding at Octavian to continue his story.

"I had been swimming and spotted a boat emptying barrels into the sea," Octavian continued. "As I got closer, I realised the barrels were full of toxic waste. One of them exploded, and the chemicals seeped into my skin, and I passed out." Ellie listened intently, horrified by the story.

"The next thing I remembered was the putrid-smelling substance leaking out into the sea. The barrels had the name Electromag on them, so I assumed the company was responsible for the dumping. As I was about to swim back to shore, the black substance encircled me. It was heavy and stuck to my legs, dragging me under the water." Ellie's eyes widened in shock at the mention of the company, Electromag, it was the one her dad worked for. She couldn't believe it.

Ellie interrupted him. "Oh, my goodness. My dad works at Electromag. He does their accounts for them. This is terrible. Is he in danger?" she asked.

Kyle quickly responded. "No, your dad, or Bill, as we call him, is not in trouble. The Underworld needs his help; it would be great if he could act as an undercover agent for us again."

Ellie raised an eyebrow, curious about Kyle's words.

"What do you mean 'again'? Has my dad helped you before?" she enquired.

Kyle continued. "Your dad used to give us vital information about Electromag's experiments. But after your mum's death, he stopped communicating with us. We understand his hesitation and have respected his decision to stay away. However, with the recent events, we believe it's necessary to ask for his help again."

Ellie felt uncomfortable when people she did not know discussed her parents. Kyle looked at her, with an eagerness to talk. Octavian chewed his lip nervously.

"We believe that Electromag is still dumping genetically modified toxic waste in multiple areas," Kyle said gravely. "It's causing a lot of damage to our planet and endangering many species. Octavian can tell you more about his transformation, if he wishes to."

Octavian took a deep breath and spoke. "It does make me anxious to relive my trauma, but I believe it's essential for you to understand why we need your help, and your dad's too."

Ellie looked down at her feet, feeling uncomfortable and avoiding eye contact. She shook her head and spoke with a determined tone. "I can only make my own decisions, and I can't speak for my dad."

"I understand. Back to my story; I panicked, thinking I was going to drown. I tried to hold my breath for as long as possible. To my surprise, I found I didn't need to; I could breathe perfectly - no gasping for air, no oxygen needed."

Ellie's eyes widened in amazement as Octavian spoke.

"That's incredible," she said, trying to sound as calm as possible. "So, you gained the ability to breathe underwater because of the toxic waste?"

Octavian nodded. "In a way, yes. I discovered I could control and manipulate water in ways I never thought possible."

Ellie couldn't help but be impressed by Octavian's abilities. She felt a sense of admiration for him and the others and knew that she had a lot to learn from them.

Octavian continued further with his explanation. "I realised that I had changed into what I now know to be a hybrid octopus."

Ellie felt a rush of emotions but was at a loss for words. She wanted to hug Octavian or say something to express her support, but the words wouldn't come out.

Octavian spoke reassuringly. "I am alright, Ellie. I have had time to adjust to my new self, and I have since confirmed that Electromag has been dumping genetically modified waste into the ocean. This changed my DNA coding to the form you see in front of you today. However, we do need your dad's help. Do you think you could convince him?"

Ellie felt a wave of stress wash over her as Octavian mentioned her dad's help was needed. It wasn't something she could casually drop during dinner conversation.

She sighed, "I'll ask him in the morning, I'm not sure he will listen, so if the message is clear and direct, it will be easier. You are aware my dad likes things to be straightforward?"

Ellie listened intently as Octavian explained in more detail.

"We need your dad to spy for us at Electromag. If we can find out when the next genetic toxic dump is, we can intercept it and hold the waste until we can dispose of it safely."

The request was straightforward, but Ellie was unsure whether her dad would be willing to participate. She nodded slowly, understanding the importance of the mission.

"I understand why you need my dad's help, but it won't be easy to convince him," Ellie said.

Octavian replied, "Trust me, if we knew another way of how to get someone else on the inside of Electromag, we would. They have stopped recruiting due to their suspicions of infiltrators. Your dad has been a loyal worker, and they won't suspect his involvement with the Underworld."

Octavian looked at her with a serious expression. "Ellie, I don't want anyone else to go through the traumatic transformation I endured. We need to stop Electromag from continuing its harmful practices. Your dad's help could make a significant difference in this fight." She was so lost in her thoughts that she didn't notice Amber until she spoke up.

"It's not just your dad's help we need, but yours too," Amber said, her voice breaking Ellie's concentration.

Ellie felt a wave of guilt wash over her. She knew that she couldn't just sit back and do nothing when so much was at stake. Her curiosity got the best of her.

"So, what kind of things can you do with your powers, Amber?" she asked.

"I can cause earthquakes, minor and major. I can make landslides happen."

"All of your powers sound quite scary," Ellie added, thinking she did not want to test her newfound powers out.

"Yes, I agree, Ellie. Thankfully, I can say I have never used them to destroy anything. I can also cause the land to become fertile so vegetation can grow at a rapid rate. If you ever want to see a demonstration of my powers and ability to grow plants, join me in the plant nursery. Come and see some of my creations," she added.

"Ellie," Octavian said, as he walked over to a drawer and retrieved a large purple envelope tied with a blue silk bow. "I have one last thing to give you." He handed the envelope to her, pausing briefly before doing so.

"When your mother's belongings were brought here, this envelope was found along with the amulet you're wearing. I didn't want to give it to you during our first meeting because I thought it was too soon. Your mother, Beth, was loved by many in the Underworld for her tireless work, and for reporting every illegal movement made by Electromag to us. We believe this led to her death." Ellie couldn't help but shiver at the mention of her mother's tragic fate.

"Your dad would pass information about Electromag to your mum, who would then alert us," Octavian explained to Ellie. "We believe Katia has found out your mum gave birth to a daughter with supernatural abilities. They don't know your identity yet, but we need to be careful." Ellie was still struggling to come to terms with the fact that she had these powers.

"Your mum instructed the Underworld that if anything happened to her, we should give you this envelope. It contains information that will alert you about the dangers you will face in the future," Octavian explained. "We will leave you in peace to read the letter. Please ring the red bell when you are finished, and Oggle Boggle will escort you to the exit. I hope you will think about the offer to help and work with the Underworld. May we meet again soon? And if you decide not to help, it has been a pleasure meeting you." Octavian turned away, hiding a look of sadness.

Ellie felt a sense of solitude in the large, old-fashioned room. She held the envelope tightly in her hand, feeling exhausted from the emotional rollercoaster of the meeting. She decided it would be best to read the letter in the comfort of her own home.

Ellie found the red bell and gave it a firm tug. The sound reverberated through the room. To her surprise, a small door opened, and out popped an out-of-breath Oggle Boggle. Despite feeling sorry for the little creature, she couldn't help but find him cute. He spoke in a soft, high-pitched voice that made her smile.

"Please, Miss Ellie, follow me, and I will take you to the exit." They left the room and headed towards a set of stairs.

"Follow the stairs upwards, Ellie. At the top, there is a hatch. Just push it up, and you will be outside. You will be next to the old oak tree. You'll be safe to walk back from there. Please return to us again, please." Oggle Boggle wobbled off down the corridor and left Ellie to walk the stairs. She did as was instructed and found herself outside.

As she walked towards the path that would lead to her home, she clutched the envelope in her hand and decided it was best not to talk to her dad about the day's events until tomorrow. First, she needed time to think and examine the contents of the envelope. The house and her dad were visible in the distance. As she approached, she noticed the worry lines etched on his face. His expression shifted from concern to relief.

"Where have you been? I've been so worried. I thought you might have been upset with me after yesterday. I didn't mean to get angry about the amulet." Her dad's voice was strained.

"I went for a walk to clear my head," Ellie lied, knowing she had to keep the truth about the envelope and Octavian's visit hidden for now. "I'm sorry for worrying you. Can we talk about it more tomorrow?" Ellie hoped her dad would believe her.

Bill smelled the air as if a familiar scent had met his nostrils. He looked around and stared at the envelope in Ellie's hand. He placed a big strong arm around her shoulder as they walked towards the house.

"Do you fancy a takeaway from Fred's chippy?" he asked.

"Real food," Ellie chuckled to herself.

***

They finished the takeaway in silence; her mind was racing with questions about the contents of the envelope, and she couldn't wait to retreat to her bed for some peace.

"That's me done for the day. I'm off to bed." She knew she wouldn't get much sleep that night, but at least she would have some privacy to open the envelope and explore its contents. Her dad kissed her on the forehead.

"Goodnight, my angel, sleep well." Ellie appreciated the gesture and knew she didn't want to worry her dad about her troubles tonight.

4

Ellie sank into her cosy bed and pulled the familiar patchwork quilt up to her chin, feeling the warmth it provided. With a trembling hand, she switched on the bedside lamp, which cast a soft pink glow over her room. Her heart was pounding in anticipation as she reached for the envelope, eager to uncover its contents.

Inside, she found several photographs of her mother, a letter addressed to her, and a USB stick. Her hands shook as she clutched the photos of her mum close to her chest. She closed her eyes, trying to hold back her tears, and took a few deep breaths to steady herself.

As she leafed through the photos, a surge of curiosity washed over her when she spotted a picture of Mr Bob Bomtane standing next to her mum.

As Ellie sifted through the contents of the envelope, a photograph slipped from her fingers and landed on the bed. It was of her mum, with a woman with strikingly beautiful violet eyes and vibrant purple hair. The name Katia was inscribed on the back of the photo. Ellie's mind raced with questions. She had heard the name Katia mentioned earlier by King Jamari.

Looking at the photos, Ellie realised she looked like a younger version of her mum- the dark hair and the way her eyes sparkled in the light. She took a deep breath, trying to steady her nerves, before carefully unfolding the letter and beginning to read.

Dear darling Ellie,

If you are reading this, I wish the situation had been different, and I would be sitting and talking with you. After seeing all this information, I hope you will understand my reasons for helping the Underworld. Without them, the Upperworld would not be able to sustain a balanced ecosystem, and there would be an increase in natural disasters.

First, let me tell you how I started working for the Underworld. When I was 20 years old, I had been helping my dad, your Grandpa Jo, at Pear Tree Farm, and that's when I met your dad. Your dad had started working at the farm, and we had such fun times and fell in love.

Back then, I was a budding young reporter, desperate to write the latest headline for the news company I worked for. My thirst for knowledge and information was unstoppable. I searched for the truth and wanted to report every injustice I found.

One afternoon, I was strolling around the farm and noticed Grandpa Jo heading towards the old barn at the end of the cow field. I had seen him go in there before and always wondered why he spent so much time there. Whenever I asked him about it, he would brush it off and say he was just clearing up clutter. But on this day, I decided to follow him.

As I got closer to the barn, I noticed that the door was ajar, so I peeped in. To my surprise, I saw Grandpa Jo working on a strange-looking vehicle. I tapped on the barn door, and he greeted me with a warm smile. He was wearing his flat cap with his glasses perched on the end of his nose, and his overalls covered his pleasantly round belly. He welcomed me into the barn.

As Ellie read the letter, she couldn't help but feel a sense of peace and connection to her mother. Settling back under the covers, she continued to read the letter.

I learned Grandpa Jo was working on a transport vehicle system called Boggopods using bioenergy. He talked about how his new transport system would help the Underworld. He told me how they needed to travel from country to country in the most environmentally effective and economically practical way. I became more and more curious about their work.

Over the years I confided in your dad about the Underworld, but he wasn't as enthusiastic as I was. Grandpa Jo had warned me about a dangerous woman involved in running the Underworld, named Katia. At the time, she was the head of the Grand Council and a zealous leader who had become corrupted by power.

Katia's goal had shifted towards destroying the Upperworld. She deemed people on the Upperworld as ignorant and responsible for destroying the planet. Several council members objected to her attitude towards humans.

When I met Katia, I found her charming but manipulative. She explained to me how the animal kingdom had suffered, and many species faced the danger of extinction. I felt I could reason with her and show her there were good people in the world who would help and fight alongside her. She wouldn't listen.

The Grand Council had kept it quiet from most in the Underworld that your dad had been spying for them and working at Electromag, including Katia. It was best no one knew, this way he could be kept safe. It was agreed your dad would never visit the Underworld, so we could keep his identity hidden. I hope this has remained the case and if so, Katia will not know of him, or you.

I became aware of how scared the Underworld members had become of Katia's behaviour. She had become obsessed with finding the 'Four Elementals' and talked about how she would use their powers to destroy humans.

I know you will now have been told by now that you are the elemental 'fire'. Thankfully, Katia doesn't know of your existence, and you have remained hidden from most of the Underworld. Bob Bomtane decided to tell only a select few in the Underworld that you had been born, and I hope this is still the case.

Ellie exhaled a deep breath, her heart racing at the thought of being hunted by the corrupt ex-leader of the Underworld. She crossed her fingers, hoping that Bob Bomtane had managed to keep her identity a secret.

The Grand Council decided the best action was to remove Katia from her position, and she was outraged. She flew into a fit, which split the Underworld into two camps. Half of the Underworld vowed to fight alongside Katia and follow her to her new stronghold.

The Underworld found out Katia planned to buy Electromag to continue dumping the chemical waste and to make it look like the humans were being careless with the planet. After hearing this, I asked your dad to film activities there, so I could report them to the mainstream media and expose their toxic crimes.

The USB shows footage of Katia discussing, with her stronghold, plans to contaminate the world, so she could blame the humans and go to war with them.

I believe Katia will make a move to go to war when all four elementals reach 16 and gain their powers, including yourself. I have instructed the Grand Council to reach out to you prior to your 16th birthday. If Katia does not control all of you, she can still use your powers, but she may not be strong enough to cause the maximum destruction she would desire.

The thought of possessing magical powers was still overwhelming to Ellie. She took a deep breath to calm herself and resumed reading her mum's words.

We were on the verge of revealing Electromag's activities to the public when Katia discovered our plans. She had me followed by a pack of shifting wolves. I thought I had evaded them, but they were too quick and followed me to my workplace. At the time, I was outside, speaking with the news company director about when to release the research I had gathered on Electromag. I had made arrangements to take my evidence on the USB to the director. The wolves eavesdropped on our conversation and reported my plans to Katia.

Katia was furious and summoned a meeting with her followers, telling them that if I went public with my information, I would ruin her plans, she feared this would stop her from rising to power. If only she had stopped to think clearly, she would have seen that we were not her enemy.

We were trying to help, to make the planet a better place, but not at the expense of killing humanity. We wanted to expose the toxic pollution and hold those responsible accountable, but Katia's hatred for humans was too intense. She didn't just want to save the planet; she wanted a planet without them.

Ellie's body tensed as she sat in the dimly lit room, clutching the letter tightly in her hand. Her mind raced with thoughts of her parents and the danger they had faced. She took a deep breath and steadied herself before inserting the USB into her laptop. As she watched the footage, her horror grew with each passing moment. She saw Katia discussing her twisted plans to destroy humanity and felt a cold shiver run down her spine.

Ellie's heart sank as the footage shifted, and she saw Katia commanding the shapeshifting wolves to hunt and kill her mum. Overwhelmed with distress, she watched the scene unfold, feeling tears welling up in her eyes. She was helpless to change the past events that were playing out before her. Exhausted from the day's events, Ellie decided to read the rest of the envelope's contents in the morning.

5

Ellie's eyelids drooped heavily, her breathing slow and steady as she slumbered peacefully. The rustling sound of the envelope being opened, and its contents examined did not stir her. It wasn't until her dad's gentle hand placed the envelope back on her bedside table that Ellie began to stir. She rubbed her eyes, disoriented and wondering why her dad was in her room so early.

"What's going on, Dad?" she asked in a groggy tone, sitting up and trying to shake off her sleepiness.

He sat down on the edge of her bed with a heavy sigh, his face bearing the weight of a grave burden. Ellie's senses heightened, and a feeling of foreboding crept up inside her as she looked at his face.

"Ellie, I need to talk to you about something important," he said in a serious tone, his voice barely above a whisper.

Ellie's heart began to race as she braced herself for what was to come.

She looked at her dad with wide, worried eyes and asked, "What is it?" in a small, trembling voice.

"I presume the Underworld wants me to come back? My answer is yes, but only to protect you." Ellie smiled in relief that the situation was resolved sooner than she had anticipated.

"Oh, Dad. I was worried about asking you."

"I can understand your concern, Ellie," her dad replied. "Did you manage to read all the contents of the envelope?"

"No, I was so tired and traumatised that I haven't had a chance to read the witness statements and newspaper articles," Ellie explained as she rubbed her eyes.

"We can go through the rest together now, if you'd like, over breakfast?" her dad offered.

"Yes, that would be better," Ellie replied. "I don't want to read about 'that day' by myself!"

As Ellie sat down at the dining room table, the tantalising aroma of vanilla pancakes topped with fresh blueberry sauce wafted into her nostrils, making her mouth water. She eagerly picked up the stack of papers in front of her and began examining the witness statements from 'that day.'

Her dad's statement to the police detailed her mum's movements, while the other accounts came from eyewitnesses. As she read through the papers, her dad began to explain his version of events, filling in the gaps and adding additional details.

"I reported in my statement that your mum had taken her usual route to work. I must be honest with you, Ellie; I chose not to mention the USB to the police, which contained evidence of Electromag's crimes and Katia's plan to kill her," he admitted, his voice tinged with regret. Ellie empathised with her dad's decision to withhold the information from the police.

"I withheld this information from the police because I couldn't mention the Underworld's involvement," explained Bill, his voice heavy with emotion. "The Grand Council had pleaded with me not to expose them. This decision weighed heavily on me, as I knew that Katia's role in your mum's death would never be uncovered." Ellie's heart sank as she bowed her head in sorrow, a heavy weight settling in her chest.

Her dad leaned back in his chair; his expression pained as he recounted the events.

"Your mum received an email from an anonymous source," he began, his voice heavy with emotion. "It contained footage, sent by an ally, of Katia planning to have her murdered. She added the video to a USB for safekeeping and included the evidence against Electromag she had gathered." Ellie listened, her heart heavy with grief and anger.

"Despite my fears for her safety and my pleas for her to stay home and contact the police," her dad continued, "your mum remained calm. She assured me Katia wouldn't risk coming to the Upperworld or sending her followers to do her bidding as it would draw attention and foil her plans."

Ellie observed the sorrow etched on her dad's face as he recounted the details of the harrowing day. He recalled the moment when her mother stood at the kitchen counter, ensuring she had put the USB evidence in her bag to take to work. Ellie could see the regret in his eyes.

"I should have stopped her."

"Dad, you can't blame yourself!" Ellie reassured him.

Her dad shook his head. "I know. I told your mum that taking the evidence to the news company could put her in danger, but she just looked at me with determination in her eyes."

Ellie could hear the concern in his voice as he continued,

"I knew that arguing with her was futile once she'd made up her mind." She could tell her mother was headstrong, and she didn't blame her dad for not being able to stop her.

Ellie's eyes widened with shock as her father recounted the events leading up to her mother's death.

"I told her to take her usual route through the park, as it was the quickest way to get there," he said, his voice heavy with emotion. "If I had known what was about to happen to your mum and that danger would be lurking in the shadows, ready to attack her, I would have gone with her."

Ellie could feel the weight of her father's grief and guilt. She reached out and placed her hand on his, offering him comfort. She could see the tears welling up in his eyes as he continued to speak.

"I should have done more to protect her," he said. "I should have insisted that she stay home and not take that risk."

Ellie knew that he had done all he could to protect her mum, and what had happened was out of his control. She picked up some more of the witness statements and read them.

Witnesses from the park had told the police about the suspicious behaviour of the women they had seen, including them crouching down next to a tree and sniffing the air. One witness found their behaviour to be very odd.

Her dad continued to give her a brief breakdown of the statement. "On the day in question, one of the eyewitnesses walked through the park and recalled seeing three women approaching her. She stated they were dressed in black, with long, dark hair. What struck her as bizarre were their fangs, which she suspected might be cosmetic. She had also noticed three wolf-like dogs. One of the dogs sensed her fear, and she said it growled menacingly at her. The witness stated she felt spooked and quickly left the park." Ellie thought how the situation must have been terrifying for the witness.

"Your mum had to take a shortcut through the quarry to her work."

Bill continued to read through the statement reports, his voice cracking with emotion as he recounted the events.

"According to the statement, the next sighting of Beth was reported by an angler at the quarry lake. The angler described feeling a sense of unease that day, as if the calm waters had transformed into a dark and foreboding abyss. He stated his peace was shattered by the sound of rocks tumbling into the water. When the angler turned to the source of the disturbance, he saw a figure moving along the narrow path at the top of the quarry, which he later identified as Beth." Her dad's voice broke with emotion as he recounted this part of the statement.

"It's alright, Dad, you can stop if you want, it's sad for me too." Bill wiped his eyes and continued.

"As with other eyewitness accounts, the man reported to the police that he had seen four women on the path, one of whom he identified as your mum. According to the statement, the man overheard their conversation clearly, and one of the women was demanding evidence on Electromag from your mum." Ellie felt a wave of anger and frustration, wishing she could have been there to protect her mother.

"The man recounted to the police the harrowing moment he witnessed your mum stumble and lose her footing on the narrow path before plunging into the dark depths of the quarry lake. Despite his best efforts to search for her, he was unable to locate her. However, he managed to retrieve her bag, which had fallen onto the rocks below."

"So how did the police not find the USB?" Ellie asked, curious about how it had been missed.

"Unbeknownst to the police, the USB was hidden deep within the lining of the bag. They returned it to me without knowing of its significance," her dad explained.

Ellie's hands shook as she reached for the stack of papers on the table. She hesitated for a moment before grabbing the newspaper article about her mum's death. As she read the words, her heart ached with sadness. She could feel the tears welling up in her eyes as she imagined the pain her mother must have gone through.

The article painted a vivid picture of the incident, describing how a young mother had drowned in the quarry lake. Ellie could almost feel the cold, murky waters closing in around her mother as she struggled to stay afloat. The article went on to say her mum's body was never recovered due to the lake's depth, leaving the family without closure.

"Do you think we will ever get justice for my mum's death?"

"I believe we will, but it won't be through conventional means. The only ones who know the truth about what happened to your mum are Katia and her pack of she-wolves. They had planned to kill her on 'that day', and her accidental fall into the quarry made it easier for them to accomplish their task." Bill looked solemn.

"After the incident, I realised I couldn't keep your mum's bag and decided to entrust it, along with the USB, to Bob Bomtane for safekeeping. I cut off all ties with the Underworld and partly held them responsible for your mum's death. My priority was your safety," her dad explained. Ellie felt relieved that her dad had put her safety first.

"I will go with Grandpa Jo tonight, to discuss with the Grand Council their plans regarding Katia. You are the only elemental who needs to reach the age of 16, and as you know, your birthday is next week."

"Do you think Katia poses a real threat to my life?"

"It is good you wear the amulet. It was made by the Underworld to protect you, on the instructions of your mum. Inside it is a tracking device that Grandpa Jo made." Her dad paused in thought. "No, I believe she poses a threat, but not necessarily to your life. She needs you alive to utilise your powers to her advantage. I think she may attempt to capture all of you and take you to her stronghold, where she will try to manipulate your abilities." Despite the conversation, Ellie didn't feel fully reassured.

"I feel somewhat safer knowing there are plans in place to track me," Ellie admitted.

"However, there is also an urgency for me to train with the elementals so I can learn to guard and protect myself." Her dad nodded in agreement. "For now, I need to focus on my homework." Ellie laughed at the mundane task, giving her dad a big hug. She knew her elemental training would come quickly.

6

Ellie shut the car door and waved goodbye to her dad. She walked to the school gates, her steps slow and reluctant. The old familiar stone school entrance loomed ahead of her. Once through the doors, the distinct smell of disinfectant and musky dampness invaded her nostrils. She took a deep breath and tried to calm her nerves.

Ellie was a straight-A student, who loved learning, but she was also bullied for being studious. The amulet around her neck pulsed, and she felt a sense of reassurance that the tracking device would keep her safe.

After the weekend's events, she felt it strange to go to school, let alone try to pretend everything was normal.

The children chatted loudly in excitement about the past weekend's events.

"Oh my god, did you go to Lucy's party on Saturday? It was such fun. I didn't see you there," one girl asked a small girl with brown hair.

The small girl shook her head. "No, I didn't go. I was sick."

"Oh, that's too bad," the girl said. "You missed out on a lot of fun."

The small girl shrugged. "I guess so."

Ellie watched the girls, their excited voices rising above the general din of the school. She hadn't known of a party, but she wouldn't have gone, even if she had known.

The shrill school bell rang out, and the pupils rushed to get to their lessons. Ellie was pushed to the side as the students hurried past. She leaned against the corridor walls, feeling the wet condensation on her hands. She waited until the bell ended before making her way to form.

The packed room was full of seated pupils, all adorned in purple and grey school uniforms. Only their hairstyles and faces distinguished them from each other. Ellie took a deep breath and tried to calm her nerves.

"Quiet, please," the voice of the teacher, Mrs Montgomery, addressed and calmed the room. "Two newcomers join us today, welcome, Amber Healey and Kyle Tunstall. I am sure you will settle during your last year at high school and be able to contribute positively," the teacher announced, her voice echoing in the classroom. The pupils turned their heads to where two unfamiliar students stood. Ellie's gaze lingered on them for a moment before recognition dawned on her. It was Amber and Kyle.

Ellie wondered if she should say hello. She glanced around the room, taking in the mixed reactions of her peers. Some looked curious, others indifferent. Ellie decided to play it safe and take a seat, her mind buzzing with anticipation for what the day might bring.

Ellie was eager to talk to Kyle and Amber, curious about their presence at her school. After the form period ended, the students headed to their first lesson.

"Sports first thing in the morning, really?" Ellie muttered to herself.

As Kyle and Amber approached Ellie, the other students began to whisper and speculate about the two newcomers.

"Does anyone know them?" one pupil asked.

"Nah, I don't. Maybe they got expelled from their last school," another replied.

The trio of Ellie, Kyle, and Amber walked away, leaving the rest of the class to continue their conjectures.

"Why are they talking to Ellie?" Emily Booth asked with a tone of suspicion, as if it were a crime for the newcomers to already know someone at the school.

"You pleased to see us?" Amber asked with a smirk.

"Oh, yes. Yes, I am." Ellie smiled, feeling the warmth of their shared group hug.

Kyle went on to explain, "The decision to place us at your school was for your protection and safety. Bill and the Grand Council had decided it was for the best."

Amber's words tumbled out in a rush as she excitedly explained the transfer. "The transfer over to this school was a breeze. Mrs Montgomery is a good friend of Mr

Bob Bomtane, and she transferred us instantly to Saint Swathing School."

Ellie felt a wave of relief wash over her as Amber linked her arm tightly with hers, reassuring her that she wasn't alone.

"Anyway, judging by the other students' response towards Kyle and me, it looks like you could do with some good company," Amber continued, the three of them sharing a laugh.

"Well, Ellie, me and you need to be off; we have sports together. Are you feeling competitive?" The mention of sports brought Ellie back down to earth, and Amber noticed her friend's concern.

"It'll be alright, Ellie. Don't worry," Amber reassured her. "I think it's cross-country today. Trust your body's energy and tune in to it," she advised, smiling at her friend. "Kyle, you have rugby, so go and enjoy it," Amber added, giving him a playful nudge.

As they walked towards the girls' changing room, Kyle gave them a wave and headed off to the boys' changing area. Ellie and Amber reached their destination, where they found most of the girls had already changed into their purple sports tops and grey tracksuit bottoms.

The PE teacher, Mrs Carlton, reminded everyone to remove all jewellery, stating it was forbidden for safety reasons. Ellie's heart sank.

'*Oh no, what am I going to do?*' she thought to herself, feeling the amulet around her neck. '*I can't take the amulet off; it'll place me in danger.*'

The girls lined up so Mrs Carlton could do a jewellery check. Ellie decided before joining the line to place the amulet in her school locker and hoped she would be safe for the next 50 minutes. Ellie could not see it had turned the deepest, dark red when she had put it in the locker; it was a warning of impending danger.

Mrs Carlton led the girls outside and arranged them into their teams at the starting line.

"Remember, girls, stay on the path, and when I blow the whistle, the race will begin," she instructed.

The girls eyed their opposing teams and eagerly waited for the signal. As soon as the whistle blew, Ellie and Amber took off running together as part of the same team.

Amber leaned over and whispered to Ellie, "You know, Ellie, if you believe in the fire inside of you, it will help you to increase your speed. Focus on the heat in your body and turn it into energy. Trust me, this will improve your ability to run."

Ellie nodded, grateful for Amber's advice. She closed her eyes and took a deep breath, feeling the warmth inside of her. She concentrated on channelling it into her legs, visualising the heat turning into energy. It was as if a vortex of energy hit her, propelling her forward. Ellie opened her eyes and ran with a newfound speed, amazed at how fast she could go.

"Wow, Amber, look, you were right!" Ellie exclaimed, but there was no reply.

She looked around and realised she couldn't see Amber or any of her team members nearby. She had run so fast that she had gone off the usual cross-country route. Ellie looked ahead. She couldn't see the figure of Katia hiding deep in the wooded area, waiting for her.

Katia was dressed in a purple velvet, hooded gown. Her hair shone with a luminous, iridescent glow. She grasped the tree with her long talons, which clawed the bark. At her side were two of her shapeshifting she-wolves in their wolf form, their fangs displayed as they snarled. They were all waiting for Ellie, who was running towards them. The amulet Ellie had left in her locker flashed black, which would have warned her of imminent danger.

***

Grandpa Jo was on his way to his shed, to work on his latest experiment when a shiver ran through his body. He looked up at the sky and saw black clouds tinged with red, a sign of an approaching storm.

"*Not good,*" he thought, "*it seems like a nasty storm is on the way.*" He quickened his pace to reach the safety and security of his shed before the storm hit.

Once inside the shed, Grandpa Jo heard the tracking device that was paired to Ellie's amulet rapidly beeping, causing him to gasp in shock. His hands were sweating with anxiety as he searched his pockets for his mobile phone. Finally, he found it and dialled Bill's number with a sense of urgency.

"Bill, Bill, it's an emergency. Ellie is in danger. Meet me at the school!" Grandpa Jo requested, feeling a knot of anxiety form in his stomach.

Grandpa Jo grabbed the tracking device and jumped into his old, battered Range Rover, driving as quickly as he could to the school gates. When he arrived, Bill was waiting for him with two members from the Underworld. Grandpa Jo felt relieved when he saw that one of the two members with Bill was Octavian. A frantic Bill paced up and down, eager to find Ellie.

"Hey, Pa. Octavian decided it best to bring along Detective Jean Marvelley; under these circumstances, she will be of great use to us. Have you got the tracking device? We need to hurry," Bill said urgently. Grandpa Jo handed him the device for safekeeping.

Bill barged through the school doors with Grandpa Jo trailing behind him, hoping they would reach Ellie in time.

"This way," Bill said as he used the tracking device to lead them to the amulet.

The smell of disinfectant overwhelmed Grandpa Jo's nostrils as they made their way down a corridor lined with lockers. But when they reached a dead end, there was no sign of Ellie. The tracking device was always accurate, so it should have led them straight to her. Jean scanned the corridor before turning to Bill with a reassuring expression.

"May I have the tracking device, Bill?" she asked politely, as she held out her hand. Bill nodded and handed over the device. Jean held it up to the lockers, analysing the signal. "I believe the amulet is inside one of these school lockers," she said with confidence.

The group didn't have to wait long as the school's headteacher arrived with two security guards.

"Is everything alright here?" the headteacher asked, looking concerned.

"We're trying to locate a missing student," Bill explained quickly. "We have traced her tracking device to being inside one of these lockers." Jean stood by Bill's side holding the tracking device.

"Leave this to me," Jean announced, as she put her hand in her pocket and pulled out an ID card.

"Hello, I'm Detective Jean Marvelley. We have an urgent situation regarding one of your students. We need this locker opened immediately. Please." One of the security men hurriedly went to find the school caretaker, returning flustered, with the caretaker, who fumbled around with a bunch of locker keys.

"Locker key number 112, please." The headteacher firmly gestured for the caretaker to open the locker.

The locker was opened, and as Detective Jean Marvelley had predicted, the amulet was inside, flashing frantically. The headteacher quickly got on his mobile phone to contact the secretary to find out which classroom Ellie was in.

"She's in a PE lesson doing cross country," the headteacher informed the group and quickly led them outside to a field. "This is the start of the cross-country field. The course goes off the beaten track, so the teams could be anywhere. Given the time of day, I would expect them to be halfway around by now."

Octavian slipped away from the group, eager to get ahead of the search for Ellie. Bill followed closely behind, his anxiety mounting as he shouted her name, his voice echoing across the field.

***

Ellie's heart raced as she ran, the wind in her face as her legs pumped like pistons, driving her forward with increasing speed. She felt alive, invigorated as if nothing in the world could stop her.

Without warning, her foot caught on a fallen branch, and she stumbled, her arms flailing for balance. For a moment, she managed to regain her footing, but then the pain hit her like a sledgehammer. Her ankle twisted, and she fell hard, hitting the ground with a thud.

She gasped, her breath coming in short, ragged bursts. She clutched at her ankle, wincing as the pain intensified. She looked around frantically, but there was no one in sight. She was alone, stranded.

"Help! Is anyone there?"

Ellie felt the throbbing pain in her ankle and knew it was swollen. It hurt when she tried to walk. In the distance, she could see three women. She shouted again and waved to attract their attention. She looked towards the three women and thought her eyes had played tricks with her. Now there was only one woman who stood there. The woman was adorned in a long purple coat with two dogs at her side. As the woman walked towards her, Ellie recognised her as Katia.

Ellie was entranced by the enigmatic Katia. As the two dogs drew nearer, their features became more wolf-like. Ellie scanned the area around her, hoping to catch the attention of another runner or spectator, but the cross-country field was deserted. Panic rose in her chest.

"*Oh no, I'm in trouble*," she tried to calm herself down. "*Stay calm, she doesn't know who I am.*"

The wolves moved towards her with menacing snarls, their hot breath filling her nostrils with a pungent scent. She could feel the hair on the back of her neck standing on end as they circled her.

"Barsheba, Narcissa, back off," Katia commanded the wolves.

They immediately obeyed, backing away from Ellie. Katia knelt beside Ellie and placed her hand on the swollen ankle. Ellie felt a warmth emanating from Katia's hand, soothing the pain in her ankle.

"You can stand now, Ellie," Katia said, her voice calm and measured. "Yes, I know your name. I make it my business to keep tabs on new members of the Underworld." Katia observed Ellie's face. "You remind me of someone I used to know." Ellie shrugged her shoulders to avoid acknowledging Katia's words.

Ellie's heart raced as she stood up, using Katia's outstretched hand for support. She couldn't believe that this woman was responsible for the death of her mum but was now helping her. Her ankle, which throbbed with pain just moments ago, now felt fine. She looked at Katia with a mixture of fear and suspicion.

"Thank you." Despite Ellie's politeness she urgently wanted to get away from Katia.

She heard familiar voices calling her name, including one she didn't recognise. Unbeknownst to Ellie, it was Detective Jean Marvelley who had joined the search party. Katia, on the other hand did recognise the voice and her expression immediately turned cold. She knew it was time to retreat, and without hesitation, she called for Barsheba and Narcissa.

"Come, we must go," Katia commanded as the wolves came to her side. "We'll meet again soon, Ellie," she said, before vanishing into the woods with her companions in tow.

Bill was the first to reach Ellie, panting and covered in scratches from the bushes he had frantically run through to get to her.

"Thank goodness you're okay," he said, relieved.

"Did Katia hurt you?" He examined Ellie, looking for any signs of injury. "Ellie, are you sure you're okay?" Bill asked, his worry not diminished.

"I'm sure, Dad," Ellie replied. "Katia helped me. She healed my ankle."

Bill looked at Ellie in disbelief. "Katia helped you. But she's dangerous, Ellie. You need to be careful around her."

"I know, Dad," Ellie affirmed, "but she didn't hurt me."

Bill shook his head. "I don't like this, Ellie. I don't like this at all." Ellie could see her dad was worried.

"She may have figured out that you are an elemental. If that's the case, she might try to make you an ally," Bill said with concern.

As he spoke, Detective Marvelley approached them.

"Hello, Ellie, I am Detective Jean Marvelley. Pleased to meet you. I am the human liaison officer working with the police. My main job is concealing incidents that occur in the Underworld that present themselves on the Upperworld."

"Hi," Ellie said, still trying to process everything that had happened.

"Please trust and believe me, Ellie. Katia is a perilous and manipulative person. I have had dealings that go so far back with her family, you would not believe it," Jean explained.

Grandpa Jo stumbled towards them, panting heavily.

"Are you alright, Pa?" Bill asked, concerned.

Grandpa Jo shook his head, still trying to catch his breath. "I just...needed a moment to rest and catch up," he said, his voice shaking.

"Katia is bad news," Jo explained. " All she wants to do is destroy. She is a sinister force. Unfortunately, she cannot be changed. It's in her blood, it is tainted with evil. Some believe there may still be some good in her from her mum's side, but few have seen it." Ellie nodded in acknowledgement of her grandpa's words, giving him a big hug.

"It's okay, Grandpa, I believe you."

"I feel the need to emphasise this message; I would never forgive myself if I did not protect another member of my family from the cruel grips of Katia," Grandpa Jo stated firmly.

"Hey, are you okay?" Kyle asked.

Ellie looked up to see Amber and Kyle with Octavian, who had managed to track them down. All Ellie could do was nod; the truth was, she felt exhausted. Running at such a speed had taken its toll and depleted her adrenaline.

"I think it's time for Ellie to have another lesson with Octavian, but for now, considering her condition, she needs to go home and rest," Kyle suggested to Bill.

The tired group huddled together and walked out of the woods to the safety of Bill's truck. Ellie sat in the back with Grandpa Jo.

"Here, Ellie, have your amulet back. I need to make a new device that you can wear all the time - one the school will not object to - but for now, it is best to put this one back on."

They stepped into the familiar surroundings of Ellie's home, and she breathed a sigh of relief. She collapsed onto the couch, her body overwhelmed from the events of the day. She glanced over at Octavian and her dad, who were deep in conversation, and wondered what new challenges she would face in her next lesson.

"Bill, I think it would be best if I stay with you for a couple of days," Octavian said. "It's nearly Ellie's 16th birthday, and I have a lot of ancient history to teach her. A few sick days from school are needed. I am sure you can clear it up with Mrs Montgomery." Ellie observed her dad's face, she knew he didn't like to invite people to stay over.

Bill hesitated, but he understood the gravity of the situation. He nodded.

"Okay, Octavian. Ellie needs all the help she can get. Make yourself at home."

Ellie felt a mixture of relief and anxiety. She was grateful for Octavian's guidance, but she wasn't sure she could handle any more secrets. She needed to rest and recover from the day's events.

"I'm off to bed, goodnight."

"Goodnight, Ellie," chimed her dad and Octavian.

So, what now, Octavian? What are you going to tell her?" Octavian's response was swift.

"Everything, Bill, with your consent, everything." Bill paced around the front room.

"I agree, Octavian, Ellie needs to know. She is no longer a baby, and I can no longer protect her from the truth." Octavian nodded in approval of Bill's honesty.

The pair sat in silence and contemplated what was to come.

7

The trusty cockerel crowed like clockwork, and Ellie woke up promptly. She descended the stairs in her pyjamas, slippers, and fluffy dressing gown. Octavian was sitting in the front room and looked fresh as a daisy. He had bathed to rehydrate himself, preparing for a busy day ahead.

"You may think the cockerel is just a normal one, but it's not," Octavian said. "In fact, it is a good starting place for today's lesson." Ellie felt relieved that she would be able to learn in the comfort of her own home.

Bill had made boiled eggs and served them in little egg cups with bunny feet and ears. Ellie couldn't help but smile, she had used these egg cups since she was a small child.

Octavian munched on his food and looked content.

"I'm thankful I can still eat normally. After my transformation, I was unsure if I would be able to. Ellie, shall we study in the lounge? It's more comfortable in there." The two made their way to the well-worn armchairs.

"Let's get back to the cockerel. When you hear its crow, what is the first thing that comes to your mind?" Ellie paused, trying to recall her thoughts.

"Usually, I think it's too early to wake up," she replied.

Octavian chuckled. "Yes, I understand how annoying it can be to be woken up early, but try to dig deeper," Octavian suggested.

Ellie let her mind wander. "If I think about it, the cockerel's crow is familiar to me. It motivates me for the day, it's like a personal wake-up call."

Octavian clapped his hands excitedly. "You're correct, well done. The crow is a wake-up call, a huge one. It's inviting you to your calling in life," Octavian explained with excitement. Ellie looked bewildered.

"Yes, Ellie, it is a cockerel, but a special one. Let me begin by telling you about the myths from Persia from thousands of years ago."

Ellie stood and stretched her legs. History was not her strong point, and she was not sure what Persian mythology had to do with her. Out of respect, she listened to Octavian, as this was her lesson.

"Scarosa is the name of the cockerel, and is a messenger sent from an ancient god named Ahura Mazda. Scarosa is calling you to join in the efforts to protect the animal kingdom and to preserve the ecological balance on Earth," Octavian explained.

"Old gods, messenger cockerels, whatever next?"

Octavian chuckled at Ellie's remark before continuing. "Katia is an enemy of Ahura, but she's not the only one. The battles between them have been going on for years, and they involve Asamara, Katia's father. He's an extremely dangerous and evil destroyer of all that is good in the universe." Ellie felt a mix of concern and fear, realising that the threat was even greater than she had thought before.

"As you know, today you met Katia, but did you know that you also met Scarosa?" Ellie looked puzzled.

"Well, yes, I met Katia, but when did I meet Scarosa? I mean, you make it sound like Scarosa is a human."

Octavian realised he needed to explain who Scarosa was. "Well, Ellie, as you know, some of the Underworld are hybrids and can change into animals. Scarosa can do this. In their human form, they are none other than Detective Jean Marvelley." In all the confusion, Ellie had forgotten she had met the detective.

"Scarosa has one purpose in life. They are bound for all eternity to stop Asamara and Katia from destroying humanity. Ahura Mazda gave her this calling, and in the Underworld, it is an honour to receive one."

"Goodness me, this goes way deeper than I could have imagined."

"Jean knows how to use their power to an elevated level in the Underworld. Therefore, when Jean approached Katia in the woods, Katia made a hasty retreat. Jean is also tasked with watching over you on the morning shift!" Octavian clarified.

"Jean is certainly multifaceted," Ellie chuckled.

"There is a big battle on the way, Ellie, between the ancient forces of good and evil in this world, and you need to be prepared. You will not be able to use your powers to their full potential until your transformation day, but I can show you how to start."

"Oh, good. I am intrigued about how I will use my powers. Up until last month, I had no idea I possessed them."

"After your transformation ceremony, you will learn how to fully use your powers, one of which will be the gift of immortality." Ellie sank deeper into the chair after this revelation; it was not what she expected to hear.

Octavian continued, "This gift of immortality is precious and envied in the Underworld. I must add that if you are injured during this coming battle, you will be able to resurrect yourself back to full health and even bring yourself back from the point of death," Octavian paused to let Ellie take the information in. "As long as it's before your last heartbeat fades into nonexistence. This is a great gift that the god Ahura Mazda has bestowed upon you for accepting their calling." Ellie looked terrified at the thought of immortality and the responsibility it would bring.

"So, I cannot die, not ever?" Ellie asked, shocked by the revelation.

"In a roundabout way, but only if you follow the rules," Octavian replied, looking worried. "You do need to be careful. You will not have immortality until after your transformation ceremony." Ellie wiped the sweat from her brow. "We panicked when you had your encounter with Katia in the woods. We feared she might kill you before you received your gift. Until then, you are not safe, and it is our job to protect you and train you to your highest capacity."

Octavian walked over to the unlit candles on the fireplace and gestured for Ellie to join him.

"Now, Ellie, take your time. Breathe calmly and focus on the candle wick. Imagine that you can ignite it with your mind, but be careful, we don't want any accidents. I don't think your dad will be pleased if you set fire to the curtains," Octavian warned.

Anticipation coursed through Ellie's veins as she faced the palms of her hands towards the candle and began to focus on the wick. She felt the heat radiating from her hands and directed it towards the candle. Light emitted from the wick, and a flame emerged. To her surprise, the flame grew bigger.

Ellie's eyes widened with excitement as she watched the flame grow bigger.

"Oh, my goodness, did I just do that?" she exclaimed, feeling the heat emanating from her hands. "It tingled in my fingertips, and then I felt a sharp pulse, almost like a tiny electric shock." She chuckled in amazement, feeling proud of her accomplishment.

Octavian walked over to her, a small smile on his lips.

"I'm glad you enjoyed the process, Ellie," he said. "The giddy feeling you felt will take about an hour to disappear. The adrenaline rush caused it, so you may start to feel tired as it wears off."

Ellie nodded, absorbing his words. She could already feel the giddiness subsiding, replaced by a sense of calmness.

Octavian continued, "We should never use our powers when enraged, as they can be used destructively. This gift will be needed when you are in battle, and you need to have great aim and control to avoid causing casualties on our side."

Ellie felt a surge of determination washing over her. She knew this was just the beginning of her training and that there was much more to learn. But for now, she felt positive and ready to face any challenge that lay ahead.

"I think with the correct training, I will gain good control."

"I need to tell you about the Div and the Deem, as they will be there in their hoards if the great battle, as rumoured, takes place. The Div and the Deem are murderous fighting beasts that move fast. You will need to aim your firepower at them, one after another. Remember, Ellie, you will not be alone in this battle. Many other skilled combat fighters will join you."

"I'm glad I won't be alone. I don't think anyone could have the power to defeat an army by themselves."

"You know, your mum tried to help Katia. She saw some good in her and believed she could show compassion. Not much is known about Katia's birth mother. Rumour has it her mother was of good spirit, but not strong enough to fight Asamara." Ellie looked sad.

"This must have been hard for Katia and her mum." Ellie knew all too well what it was like to grow up without a mum. She felt blessed to have been lucky to have a dad who loved and nurtured her.

"History tells us Asamara bullied Katia's mum into hiding, fearing for her life. Sadly, the system of the Underworld to protect victims had become as corrupt as its leaders." Ellie was beginning to understand why Katia had turned out to lack compassion towards others.

"Well, my mum did have a point. Katia helped me in the woods yesterday. She healed my ankle, and I didn't feel fearful that she would kill me. I felt fear from her wolves, but who wouldn't?"

"Please don't be misled. I believe she would not hesitate to kill. You are correct, though; if she knows you are one of the elementals, then she would not harm you. Katia struggles to control her temper, so even if she does need to manipulate you for your power, her hot-headedness may get the better of her."

Octavian stopped speaking. Ellie had become transfixed on an object in the room. Octavian followed her gaze towards a large eyeball suspended in the room. He put his head down to avoid eye contact with the eyeball and addressed it.

"Egor the Eye, I haven't seen you in a long time, excuse the pun. What are you doing here, spying on us? Who sent you?"

The eyeball did not respond, as Egor could not communicate verbally. Octavian waited and watched as a projected image was cast on the floor. He was being careful not to look directly at Egor to avoid falling into the transfixed state Ellie had found herself in.

The projected image revealed an ancient castle perched on a towering hill, surrounded by a dense forest. The castle's walls were weathered and overgrown with ivy, hinting at the many years it had stood. As the image zoomed in, it showed a small group of people entering the castle's grand entrance.

The image flickered, and the view changed to the inside of the castle's dining hall. A large mahogany table stood in the centre, covered with an elaborate feast of food and drink. The group that had entered were now seated around the table; their expressions were intense as they looked at each other.

The door creaked open, and a tall man with a muscular physique walked in. He stood over six feet tall and had long black hair, tied back neatly, complementing his handsome, clean-shaven face. Dressed smartly in a black tailored suit, he looked striking to the eye. A large wolf with piercing blue eyes followed him closely, staying by his side. He strode confidently to the head of the table and commanded the attention of the seated group.

"Silence, my friends. Let me introduce myself. I am Ahriman, the creator of many dangerous creatures. I control these creatures; they are mine. I made them and whatever my will is, they do it."

The group fell silent and fixated on this imposing figure before them. Everyone in the room had heard of him, and some had encountered him before. Asamara, who was one of the guests, stood up to greet Ahriman. They had both collaborated in the past, wreaking havoc wherever they went.

Asamara was a gangly, scrawny man with a scruffy beard and pointed features. His chin jutted out slightly, and his beady eyes gave off a cold, calculating stare. At first glance, one might have thought him harmless, but his mind was sharp and powerful, coupled with a complete lack of empathy for anyone else.

***

Octavian studied the projected image that Egor displayed. He knew that this was not good, and it indicated nefarious plans were being made. The image continued to reveal the events in the castle room, including the next guest at the table, Jahi, who was the on-again-off-again companion of Ahriman.

Jahi sat at the table, dressed in a black outfit made entirely of raven feathers. Her hair, black as coal, was pulled back tightly into a neat bun. Her eyes, also seemingly black, were something she prided herself on. With youthful skin and deep, blood-red lips, Jahi looked imposing as she nonchalantly examined her long nails. A scratch from her nails would release a venom strong enough to induce 24 hours of sleep or, worse yet, kill the victim.

The next person to take a seat at the table was Vidatu, known to others as the 'Demon of Death', and Ahriman's assistant. No human had ever escaped Vidatu's death grip. If he captured them, their screams of terror would ring out into the air. Throughout his history working for Ahriman, he had never shown mercy to his victims. Octavian shuddered as he viewed Vidatu.

Vidatu's broad shoulders were squared as he took a seat at the table, his spine stiff and his head held high. A small smirk hung at the corner of his lips. His black velvet hooded cloak hung heavily on his frame; the soft material brushed against his skin as he shifted in his seat. The golden clasp, fashioned in the shape of a skull, glinted in the dim light of the room, a stark reminder of the death that followed in Vidatu's wake.

Octavian watched in shock as Vidatu opened his mouth, emitting a swirling green vapour that filled the room like a plume of smoke. The vapour coiled around Vidatu like a sinister serpent, as if it were alive and feeding off his dark energy.

A loud crash broke the silence, and the heavy wooden door swung open. In walked a strange creature with three heads, each one snarling and baring its teeth. Octavian's heart raced as he realised that this was no ordinary creature - it was something otherworldly, something beyond his wildest nightmares.

With a prideful tone, Ahriman welcomed Dazi Haka. "Welcome, my fiercest battle creature. I am immensely proud of this fighting machine," he declared. "His ability to create maximum damage by breathing fire is inconceivable. As I said before, my creations are under my control and command. Watch this."

Ahriman turned towards the creature; he commanded it to be at ease. Octavian watched in awe as the beast began to shake and transformed into three plump men joined at the shoulders. They had round, chubby faces with identical features, and each wore a quizzical expression.

The three-headed men whispered to each other, then simultaneously trudged their way towards the couch and clumsily sat down. The guests gasped, applauded, and chatted frantically with each other. One woman in the group was heard above the others; this was Morag the Hag. Morag shrieked loudly with laughter and clapped repeatedly.

Morag was taken aback by the creature and couldn't help but exclaim, "Divine, simply divine creature. Oh, I would love one of these for a pet."

Ahriman interrupted her, banging his fist on the table and extending his finger to silence her with a bellow, his voice sharp with anger.

"Never call Dazi Haka a pet; it is an insult to a creature far more superior to your fading talents, Morag." As he spoke, the air in the room thickened with a ghastly, hideous smell that made everyone's eyes water. A strange, eerie, orange mist swirled and twirled around the room.

The guests looked around in alarm as the mist grew thicker, obscuring their view of the room. They could barely see each other through the eerie glow, and the smell was making them feel sick. A loud bang shook the room and the mist cleared as quickly as it had appeared. Octavian watched in shock.

The seat where Morag the Hag had sat was now empty.

"Be at ease, my guests. Morag will return when she has calmed down and display more of her hidden talents. Once a witch, always a witch," Ahriman stated with a sly grin.

***

Once the belle of the ball, Morag the Hag had the power to manage to turn the heads of many a male and female. But now, at 1,000 years old and with faded powers, she had lost her charm. Her once-youthful face had been her weapon. People used to say that one look from Morag would scramble your brain for up to a week. These days, she was lucky to get a person to even glance her way.

As she aged, Morag's appearance had transformed her into that of a hag, and with it, her confidence had waned. Morag had given herself the moniker 'Morag the Hag,' a title that suited her haggard face. A pronounced hump on her shoulders added to her unseemly appearance. If Morag had been kinder to herself, she would have realised for a witch from her bloodline, she had fared well to reach 1,000 years old.

Ahriman had summoned her because he believed Morag was still a valuable and formidable ally to have in battle. Although she couldn't change her appearance as much as she used to, she could still manage the occasional day of magical youth and beauty.

Morag mused to herself after she disappeared from the meeting, "No one treats me badly. I'll show them that they can't do battle without me," she muttered as she hid in the shadows.

Ahriman had been right; despite her age and fading powers, Morag was still cunning, vindictive, and useful in battle. Just last week, rumours had circulated that a beautiful woman had stolen the heart of the extraordinarily successful billionaire business tycoon, Terry Trueman. Terry was known for his past statements that no woman would marry him for his money. So, it came as a shock to his few genuine friends and business associates when he announced he was getting married.

When questioned, Terry gave the same vague answer, "Morag is the one for me." Some in the same business arena thought Terry had been put under a spell by a money grabber.

Using magic and glamour spells, Morag had transformed herself into a curvaceous, blonde temptress. She had managed to swindle him out of millions. Despite the police having circulated pictures of her, no one had ever seen the woman before and couldn't help the tycoon track her down to bring her to justice.

Morag had only created the persona of the blonde woman seconds before meeting Terry. She never kept the same face twice, which ensured she would never get caught. This cunning behaviour was precisely why Ahriman had invited her as a guest.

***

Octavian watched intently as Egor shut down the beam without warning.

"Egor, please show me the rest of the meeting," Octavian requested.

As swiftly as the eyeball appeared, it vanished. Egor was nothing but a mere hologram with the ability to hypnotise you with its gaze, to then leave you in a dormant state; this is what Ellie had endured.

As Ellie started to come around, she groaned and rubbed her forehead, and tried to make sense of what had happened.

"Why do I feel so disoriented?" her voice trembled with confusion.

Octavian looked at her with concern. "You were under the influence of Egor's hypnotic beam. We need to act fast and call an urgent meeting with the Grand Council."

Ellie nodded in agreement and the two of them made their way to the Underworld, where they hoped to find Bob Bomtane. As they walked, Octavian couldn't shake off the feeling of dread that had settled in his stomach. He knew Ahriman was an expert manipulator and it was impossible to predict his motives. Nevertheless, Octavian knew Ahriman would not be on their side and that they faced a dire situation, one the Underworld could not afford to ignore.

8

Octavian arrived at the grand hall and tugged on a long cord hanging from the ceiling. A bell resounded with a loud, prolonged peal. Within a few minutes, Oggle Boggle appeared before him.

"How may I be of assistance, Master Octavian?"

"Oggle, could you please bring Bob Bomtane and as many council members as you can find? It's an emergency," Octavian urgently requested.

The hall was filled with the sound of members of the council as they hurried to their seats. The gavel hit the table, and Bob Bomtane stood up and addressed the room.

"Order, order!" Bob called out. The room fell silent as everyone waited to hear the reason for their urgent summons. He motioned for Octavian to come to the front of the hall. "Octavian, please share with us what you witnessed," Bob Bomtane requested.

Octavian nervously stepped forward, addressing the small crowd that had assembled at such short notice. He took them step by step through what Egor's eye had projected onto the floor and explained how Ellie was trying to regain her focus after being in a hypnotic state.

Ellie had attended the meeting with Octavian, her face filled with despair. She seemed unable to form coherent responses, indicating she was still in a compromised state.

"So, do you think this band of undesirables are going to join Katia and her plans for a great battle?" Bob asked.

Octavian looked pained, realising he had to admit this harsh reality. "Sadly, yes I do," he admitted with a heavy heart.

"If this is the case, they are escalating their plans and creating a fierce set of creatures and formidable allies to help them." The room fell silent as the gravity of the situation sank. Bob acted decisively.

"I am going to announce a week of emergency planning and advanced training for all participants eligible for battle. I will send this notification out to all that cannot be present today and to the far corners of our planet, above and below." The members of the hall hung their heads in silence.

"Please go home to your families and prepare," Bob said, his voice heavy with the weight of the impending battle. "The months ahead will be tough, and we may sadly lose loved ones. The sooner we train for combat, the better prepared we'll be."

Octavian looked over at Ellie and noticed the exhaustion etched on her face. He placed a comforting hand on her shoulder as Bob gave his instructions.

"Octavian, take Ellie back home," Bob said firmly. "She's in no fit state. In the morning, when she's refreshed, gather Kyle and Amber and return here to start your training."

Octavian nodded in agreement and turned to Ellie.

"Come on," he said gently. "Let's get you home and rested." Ellie nodded, grateful for his support.

Octavian contacted Bill for a ride home, as Ellie struggled to walk. When Bill arrived, he looked rightfully concerned.

"Octavian, do you think Ellie can cope with this? You are young too but more familiar with the history of the Underworld." Octavian showed no offence to Bill's words, he understood that the coming battle would be difficult for any parent to come to terms with.

"Sadly, Bill, I don't believe we have a choice but to prepare. If we don't, the consequences could be disastrous." Octavian's words were met with a softening of Bill's expression.

"Octavian, I know you are wise beyond your years, but it is my responsibility to guide and support you, along with the other elementals, to become the best versions of yourselves," Bill declared.

As they walked through the dimly lit corridors of the Underworld, Octavian couldn't help but notice the energy in the air. The sound of clashing swords echoed, as a testament to the abundance of talent and combat expertise that resided within the walls. The Underworld had a hotbed of warriors, and with the looming threat, there was no shortage of individuals ready to assist with the battle.

An unprecedented army was on the verge of being formed, a force like no other. As they reached their destination, Bill turned to Octavian, his eyes filled with determination.

"We must prepare Ellie for her 16th birthday and her transformation day; we need her to be ready for what's coming."

Octavian nodded in agreement, fully aware of the weight of the task ahead. Octavian couldn't help but feel a sense of urgency. This was their chance to train, to become the best versions of themselves and to create an army that would fight to save humanity.

9

Ellie woke up on the morning of her 16th birthday and ran to her bedroom mirror and examined her face.

"*Hmm, well, I still look the same*," she thought to herself.

Ellie had imagined that her appearance would have magically changed on her birthday. She would change, just not yet.

As she was lost in thought, her bedroom door creaked open, and Grandpa Jo and her dad shouted, "Happy Birthday, Ellie!"

They aimed party poppers into the air, startling Ellie with the loud bang, but she was excited, nonetheless. She ran over to them and hugged them tightly. Today was going to be a day full of celebration for her, hosted by the Underworld.

The grand hall was a remarkable sight, adorned with large garlands of red, green, and gold that hung from the ceiling. Tables and chairs had replaced the usual seating arrangements, each with beautiful floral centrepieces. The aroma of the food from the splendid banquet filled the room, enticing the senses of everyone.

The attending crowd wore either white gowns with red sashes around their waist or white tailored suits with red cravats. Even the animals that could not shape-shift had white and red bows around their necks, to add to the festive atmosphere.

The crowd chatted merrily as they awaited the transformation ceremony. Bob Bomtane had carefully selected the best security personnel for the occasion, to prevent any unwelcome guests from disrupting the ceremony. Kyle was on high alert and scanned the hall for any unfamiliar faces. Meanwhile, the band played an upbeat tempo, and several guests took to the dance floor to enjoy the festive atmosphere.

Ellie sat quietly in the meditation room and imagined what lay ahead. She had not known what to expect but had vowed to act responsibly, knowing people and animals relied on her. As Grandpa Jo and her dad entered, Ellie opened her eyes. They looked smart in their white suits. Bill held out his hand to assist his daughter in standing up.

"Ellie, you look beautiful. The hall is ready, and everyone is waiting. How do you feel? Are you nervous?" Ellie stood up and hugged her dad.

"Yes, Dad, I am nervous. I don't know what to expect."

"Everything will be fine; this is your destiny. I cannot remove your fear, but Grandpa Jo and I will support you."

Grandpa Jo watched his granddaughter, sadness tinged his face. "You look beautiful. It is sad your mum can't see you today," he said.

Ellie stood there in her white dress, sporting the same red sash as everyone else. Her long black hair cascaded over her shoulders. The red garland headdress matched her ruby-red lips.

"Come, we better meet my waiting guests."

The hall echoed with the sound of clapping as she entered. Ellie felt embarrassed, and her cheeks blushed. In the centre of the hall stood a large stone firepit that had not yet been lit. Ellie spotted Kyle, Amber, and Octavian seated behind the firepit; the trio smiled at her. She admired how beautiful they all looked.

"Come on, let's go join them," she said to her dad and Grandpa Jo.

Bob Bomtane stood next to an elaborate, gold-gilded chair. He beckoned her.

"Ellie, please be seated upon this throne that has been made fitting for a queen."

She remained silent, partly due to her nerves, and proceeded to sit on the throne. Bob Bomtane coughed and cleared his throat to speak.

"May I welcome you all on this wonderful evening and, of course, the transformation ceremony for Ellie." Cheers filled the room.

"Many of you may have seen a transformation ceremony before, but you have never seen a fire transformation ceremony because this is the first one. I can assure you we are all in for an interesting and enlightening evening," Bob said, causing Ellie to look panic-stricken.

"If you're not familiar with the history, or should I say legend, let me give you a briefing," Bob

Bomtane announced to the audience. "We have many ancient books and records in the library housed in the Underworld. However, the book 'The Fire Bird Transformation' has been missing from the library, presumably stolen. The book talks about the one who can complete this process. We believe the book is being kept in the Forbidden Underworld under lock and key, but enough information has been passed down, through word of mouth."

Ellie's face contorted with fear.

"*So, they're telling me they have no idea how this transformation process works? Great, is it even safe?*" Her expression conveyed her panic to the room.

"Ellie, I know you are scared, and perhaps my words about the book being stolen from the Underworld were inconsiderate," Bob said. "But word of mouth in the Underworld is deemed just as reliable as the book itself. We have oral translators trained to recite the information safely, should a book fall into nefarious hands."

There was a sigh of relief not just from Ellie, but the whole room. Bob continued to explain what the legend of the firebird entailed.

"From our translations, we know that this will be the last group of elementals to grace the planet." Gasps echoed around the hall.

"They will save the planet. Each elemental has extra unique gifts. Ellie's gift is the 'Firebird' transformation. As for Octavian, we know he is a hybrid, but we are unsure about Kyle and Amber, as it has not yet been revealed." Kyle and Amber glanced at each other with worry etched on their faces.

"The process itself does sound dangerous, and we hope it will not scare Ellie off from completing it," Bob explained. Ellie felt a sense of trepidation.

"I sense your fear, and I will try to speed up the ceremony before you call the whole thing off," Bob said as he urged Ellie to stand by the firepit with him.

"Ellie, you have been undergoing secret training and have already become a master at working with fire, controlling, and manipulating it. This transformation will not be harder than the training you have already undergone. Believing in yourself will keep you from harm," Bob reassured her.

Ellie's thoughts turned to the potential possibility of death. She took a deep breath and prepared for what lay ahead as she walked toward the now lit fire pit.

Ellie felt the heat from the flames hit her face, causing her to feel nauseous.

"Right, focus, you got this girl; you can do it," she reminded herself.

She remembered the grounding techniques she had learned to help her focus. She knew that the aim was to turn the flame from the orange colour it glowed to a purple hue.

Ellie's eyes remained fixed on the centre of the flame as she visualised it changing to a deep purple. She took a deep breath and extended her hands towards the flame and focused all her energy on the task at hand. As she concentrated, the heat emanating from the flame seemed to wane. Slowly but surely, the flame began to lose its orange colour and transform into a radiant white before it settled on a rich shade of purple.

The crowd erupted in applause. Ellie basked in the warmth of their admiration. Her dad and Grandpa Jo shouted words of encouragement, which added to her sense of accomplishment.

"You go, Ellie. That's my girl!" Ellie's dad exclaimed with pride. Ellie smiled, feeling more at ease to complete the transformation.

"Well done, Ellie," Bob praised. "You know the next part. Please step into the purple flame. It will not harm you, as you have done the alchemical process correctly." He ushered her towards the flame.

Ellie climbed the concrete steps with a sense of panic. As she approached the firepit basin, the purple flame beckoned her forward with its calming glow. She glanced back at the crowd and with a deep breath, she took the last step into the flame.

The iridescent centre of the flame surrounded her as it danced and flickered around her body. Ellie's senses were heightened as she absorbed the warmth and energy of the fire. She could feel the heat from the flame, but it was not uncomfortable.

Suddenly, everything went black. Ellie was enveloped in a deafening silence. Panic threatened to take over her body, and just as she was about to give up a voice spoke to her, breaking the eerie silence.

"Ellie, once the transformation process is complete, you must go to the Oracle through the white door. Bob Bomtane will guide you there. This will be your next mission. But before this, you must experience a brief death to be reborn."

Ellie couldn't see who spoke, but she could feel the heat from the flame as it intensified. Sweat dripped off her brow as she struggled to catch her breath. The flame's colour shifted back to orange, and Ellie found herself unable to see the crowd. She was overcome with fear.

Ellie's hand trembled as she watched it turn charred black. As the heat of the flames increased, it lapped around the bottom of her dress. She should have been writhing in agony, but she felt nothing but a strange numbness. Her mind went blank, and she lost consciousness.

Ellie lay curled up in a ball on the ground motionless as flames continued to engulf her. The audience in the hall gasped and shouted in shock, their faces twisted in horror. Bill rushed over to his daughter's side, but there was no response from her. She was completely still, with no breath, no movement, and no heartbeat. She was gone.

"Help her." Bill's desperate plea was etched on his face as he watched his daughter as she lay on the floor. Without hesitation, Amber, Kyle, and Octavian rushed over to assist.

A voice boomed throughout the hall. "Silence, please. No hysteria. Wait," commanded Bob Bomtane with a raised paw.

The flame came to a standstill. Ashes were scattered on the floor where Ellie had been lying. Movement could be seen within them as bits of ash started to float upwards.

A vortex swirled up and formed a human shape. The ashes began to transform into a solid mass, and soon a figure glowing red emerged. The once white dress was now a dark shade of red, encrusted with crystallised embers from the fire that shone like diamonds. The crowd gasped in amazement as they realised Ellie had arisen from the fire like a phoenix.

"Welcome our new 'Queen of the Underworld!'" A loud cheer erupted and echoed throughout the hall. Ellie felt awkward being the centre of attention but took a bow and acknowledged their cheers.

"Ellie, you have been to the realm of the 'Valley of Death' and survived to be resurrected. You now have immortality," Bob exclaimed. Unfazed by her transformation, Ellie needed to share the message she received in the fire.

"When I was in the flames, a voice spoke to me and told me that after the transformation was complete, I needed to find them. The voice said that you would show me the white door that leads to the Oracle," Ellie explained. Bob listened intently.

"Yes, I can show you the door but please enjoy the banquet first, then I will take you there," Bob replied. Ellie tried to enjoy the rest of the festivities, but her mind remained focused on the next part of her mission, the encounter with the Oracle.

10

Ellie stood before the white door, which appeared ordinary with no gilded door handle or letterbox to distinguish it.

"I will see you soon, Bob," she said before turning her attention to the door's simple plaque that read 'The Oracle'. Ellie knocked on the door.

"Enter." The command was the same voice from the flame.

The Oracle sat suspended in space. Her pure white hair was set against her pale skin and her lips were tinged with blue. Ellie thought she looked both beautiful and surreal. Standing before the Oracle, Ellie didn't know what to do. She was about to speak when the Oracle opened her dark, black eyes. They had no pupils, only blackness. The Oracle wore a flowing white dress that moved as if it were alive.

"Thank you for coming to see me," said the Oracle. "You can ask one question today and take one item with you. Choose carefully because one day this item may save your life." Ellie felt confused as there was no item in sight.

"Hurry, I have limited time in this space. I have to move continuously so no one can find me and exploit my forever-knowing knowledge," urged the Oracle.

Ellie walked over to her apprehensively and held out her hands. The Oracle hovered in the air and took

Ellie's hands, causing a warm, tingling sensation to run throughout her body. Ellie asked her question.

"Will I be able to save the earth and its inhabitants from the destruction caused by the evil forces at work?"

Ellie looked into the black abyss of the Oracle's eyes. The Oracle took a deep breath and exhaled. As it did, a warm, misty heat surrounded Ellie. When the mist cleared, she couldn't see the Oracle anymore.

Ellie felt like she was in a void, with only her thoughts running through her head. She didn't understand where her answer was. She observed her surroundings and realised she was still in the white room, her hands clenched together and tingling. Carefully, she opened her hands and examined the visible contents. In one hand was soil, and in the other was a bag of seeds.

Ellie placed the loose soil into the bag of seeds, presuming that the Oracle had given them to her for later use. She sealed the package tightly and secured it in her pocket. Ellie had expected the Oracle to give her a prophetic message about the earth's outcome, but instead, she was left with the task of planting and growing the seeds. With no one coming to her aid, she made her way to the door. As she opened it, she was amazed to find herself in a room that was a stark contrast to the simple white room she had just left.

Ellie was immediately hit by the musty smell of old objects as she stepped into the dimly lit room.

She squinted, as it took a few moments for her eyes to adjust after leaving the brightly lit room with the Oracle. The room was part of an old antique shop, and it was filled to the brim with objects. While there were the usual chairs, lamps, and tables that one would expect to find in a shop of that calibre, there was nothing ordinary about this particular store.

Feeling tired, Ellie decided there was no harm in sitting down on one of the available chairs to rest for a little while. No sooner had she settled into the high-backed chair than she fell asleep, only to be awakened by a gentle voice speaking to her.

"Am I what you want? Are you comfortable? Would I look good in your room? You can take me home if you want."

Ellie opened her eyes and looked for the sales assistant who was talking to her, only to realise it was the chair speaking. Startled by the revelation of a chair speaking and trying to sell itself, she stood up, looked around, and heard that she was not alone; someone else was in the room with her. A hearty laugh was coming from behind the high shop counter.

"Hello and welcome. Over here. May I be of assistance?"

Ellie walked over to the shop counter, peered over it, and was more than pleased to see a tiny, elderly elf smiling back at her, laughing. Ellie did not share his amusement, and the elf-man could see this. He extended his hand as a welcoming gesture.

"Welcome to the 'One Thing and One Thing Only' shop, where you may take and keep for free, one item to help with your trials and tribulations ahead. I apologise for the chair's behaviour. The chair has been here for 100 years and has taken it upon itself to become its own salesperson to leave the shop. It happens when objects get bored being in one place only. However, let's move on from that. My name is Wilbur, and I am the owner of this shop. How may I assist you?" Ellie felt reassured by Wilbur's explanation and shook his hand to show her gratitude.

The cuckoo clock struck one o'clock and chimed, "Take me too."

Ellie laughed at the clock trying to sell itself.

"If you stay here long enough, they will all ask you to take them home. You should think quickly, your time is running out. Think wisely and only take the one item your intuition tells you to take," the shopkeeper instructed.

Ellie struggled with the heat and stuffiness in the shop. She felt anxious as there were so many items available. What if she didn't choose correctly? Objects tried to entice her. She could have sworn a group of army officers in an old black and white framed photograph were beckoning her over.

Ellie diverted her attention away from the photograph to a jug of water on the counter.

"May I have a drink of water, please? I'm so thirsty," Ellie asked.

100

"Of course, here's a glass," Wilbur replied. The heat in the shop was making Ellie feel flustered, and she hoped a cool drink would help calm her. She gulped the water down.

"Well done, Ellie. A wise choice, if I say so myself."

"What do you mean? I haven't chosen anything yet," Ellie looked dismayed.

"Just by merely drinking the water means you have chosen it as your item. The rules of the shop state 'one thing and one thing only'. I assure you, young lady, you and the water have chosen each other well. Please do not be mistaken, items in the shop will use all means to entice you to pick them."

Ellie noticed the room temperature had returned to normal, and she felt refreshingly cool. However, she also felt cheated by the sales techniques used in the shop.

"That's not fair at all."

"You can file a complaint if you like." The shopkeeper pointed to a large stack of completed complaint forms and handed Ellie a blank form.

"Just add it to the pile when it's completed. I must warn you that the waiting time for a complaint review is at least 100 years from now, if you wish to proceed. Otherwise, could you please leave my shop as I need to close for dinner? I'll be back in 10 years. If you ask me, it's a reasonable length of time for my dinner break. Or would you like to complain about that too?"

Ellie shook her head. "No, thank you."

She couldn't help but think that he was rude as she made a hasty retreat and bid him farewell.

11

Ellie found herself on an old, cobbled path with a wooded area on each side. A sign read, '*Bluebell Woods, 2 miles ahead*'. The small print stated that the land was restricted and protected, belonging to Lady Marabelle.

Ellie had no idea where she was heading, but she continued towards Bluebell Woods, hoping for a chance to get help from Lady Marabelle. As she walked, the path through the woods seemed endless. She caught a whiff of a sweet floral scent, and up ahead, she saw volumes of blue flowers. The sound of bells chiming was accompanied by angelic singing from a choir that echoed through the air. As Ellie got closer, the chimes and singing became louder, as if a choir of 1,000 people were all singing in pure harmony.

Ellie heard giggling and sensed someone watching her. A sound emanating deep vibrations was coming from the bluebells. The vibration level was so strong, it gave Ellie goosebumps all over her body as if an electrical energy force had surrounded her. She felt she was in a trance as the sound began beating in perfect sync with her heartbeat.

She stopped in the middle of the bluebells and noticed it was now eerily silent, with no more beating or chimes. Ellie felt the wind blowing around her. The wind gently whispered her name.

"Ellie, come closer. Come closer to the bells, join us in the woods," whispered a voice from within the bluebells. Ellie wondered if someone was sitting in the field watching and beckoning her. The wind whispered her name again, urging her to approach the bluebells.

"Ellie, Ellie." She spun around and sensed someone behind her and jumped when she saw a man standing there. "Sorry, I didn't mean to make you jump. My name is Blue. Pleased to meet you." Blue held his hand out to Ellie.

"I am a spirit worker and I work with the surrounding ether to receive messages from the universe. I used the breeze to whisper your name," Blue said, looking rather pleased with his skills. Ellie thought it best to acknowledge him with a smile.

"Nice to meet you, Blue. I'm a bit lost and I need to return to the Underworld. Can you help?"

Blue chuckled. "Well, it's funny you should ask. I am a spirit guide aided by the ancient knowledge of the world, so I can assist you." The chiming and singing resumed.

"Can I ask where the singing is coming from?" Ellie enquired.

Blue let out a deep, hearty laugh before answering, "It's coming from Lady Marabelle's bluebells. They sing every day as a token of their gratitude. You see, Lady Marabelle campaigned to protect the bluebells in the wood, and they see her as a bit of a saviour. She stops them from being destroyed."

The sound of the bluebells was indeed delightful, and as if on command, they all chimed and started singing. Ellie clapped joyously and thanked the bluebells.

"Blue, my second question is: does Lady Marabelle have a house nearby? I need to rest and try to contact some of my friends. Do you think it's possible?"

Blue paused, licked his finger, and extended it into the air. "Ellie, the wind is blowing in a northeast direction, so we need to head that way. Lady Marabelle always moves her cottage in the direction of the wind to help pollinate her flowers. You will find her most welcoming. She is a frequent visitor to the Underworld; Octavian is remarkably close to her."

Ellie and Blue bid farewell to the bluebells and started walking.

"How will we find Marabelle's cottage if we don't know where she placed it?"

Blue bent down and picked up two sticks, handing them to Ellie. He then collected some dry bracken and cupped it in his hands.

"Now, Ellie, a lesson in the old ways; please rub the sticks together very fast over my hands."

She did this and watched the tiny spark land on the bracken. Blue cupped his hands together and slowly blew into his hand. Ellie watched with amazement as large smoke rings rose into the sky.

"Ellie, we have now contacted Lady Marabelle. All we must do is watch for the bubbles she sends and follow them." No sooner had the smoke signals ascended into the bright blue sky than two large translucent bubbles appeared above them.

"Come on, follow the bubbles; my estimation is Marabelle's cottage is only about a three-minute walk."

The air was filled with the sweet aroma of homemade baking, a mixture of sweet cookies and fudge chocolate. As Ellie and Blue turned the corner, they were greeted by a freshly painted picket fence surrounding a beautiful garden. The garden boasted over a hundred varied species of plants, including fruits, vegetables, and flowers. The gate was adorned with wooden carved bluebell flowers at the top. Blue opened the gate, and they walked up a white stone gravel path towards the stunning stone cottage.

The cottage had a charming, thatched roof and smoke rose from the chimney, carrying the delightful aroma of cinnamon. The path leading to the cottage was lined with bluebells that gently chimed a soothing tune. Ellie admired the sun shining on the circular stained-glass windows, decorated with intricate designs. Before she could examine them further, Blue knocked on the ornate arched door.

The door opened, and they were greeted with a cheerful welcome.

"Hello, dears, do come in. I was just about to send out more bubbles, but there's no need now."

Lady Marabelle gestured for them to sit on a large floral two-seater sofa. Ellie felt instantly at home and took a liking to Lady Marabelle, a cheerful woman with a mass of curly red hair. She was dressed in a tweed suit paired with brown walking boots and held an exceptionally large Calabash pipe in her hand. Ellie noticed that every now and then, an odd bubble would rise out of the pipe.

Lady Marabelle paced back and forth in front of Ellie and Blue. "I don't like to sit down much. I'm always tending to my plant babies," she said. A loud, shrill buzzing noise pierced their ears.

"That is the greenhouse plants and vegetables crying; they need watering. Would you both like to come with me? They're in the back garden. We can grab a watering can on the way out and talk while we water them. Don't be afraid of the bees; they won't sting you. They're rather cuddly and friendly."

Ellie felt uneasy about going out into the garden with the bees, as they were not her favourite insect. She looked at Blue, who seemed unfazed. As they approached the back door, Ellie could already hear the loud buzzing. Lady Marabelle turned to her.

"Here's your watering can, Miss Ellie. Get ready for a beautiful treat."

As Lady Marabelle opened the door, a sweet fragrance filled Ellie's nostrils, and she let out a gasp of surprise. In front of her was a miniature version of the Amazon rainforest. A significantly large bee greeted her, followed by approximately 100 more. Ellie screamed at the sight of them. The bees were 15 inches long with big, fluffy bodies.

"It's alright, Ellie. Stay calm. They're only coming to welcome you. I promise you they've never stung anybody, except for people or creatures that have tried to harm them. This is Queen Beatrice." The bee hovered in front of Ellie before coming to rest on her shoulder.

"Hello, Ellie, we are so glad we could meet you. There was a rumour buzzing around our hive that you would be visiting here today. I am here to tell you we are all here at your service. Should you ever need to create an army to defend the Underworld, I have an army of highly trained fighting bees. They are the elite Honey Unit, prepared to die in honour of saving and protecting their species. Their sting is lethal, and no one can survive it, and there is no antidote." The 100-strong army of honeybees lined up impressively in front of Ellie.

The bees presented Ellie with their stingers, which were at least five inches long and looked like stainless-steel knives. The Queen bee instructed Ellie to hold out her hands, and although hesitant, she complied. Queen Beatrice flew down and hovered over her hands, allowing Ellie to stroke her. The

Queen bee felt fluffy and gentle, and her fear dissipated.

"I hope this has helped you realise that we mean you no harm. We are not your enemies, but your friends. And when you need us, just hum, and the vibration of your voice will call us. For now, we will depart; we have pollination work to do. As you have seen, Lady Marabelle is a busy woman, preserving and creating habitats, and developing new species," the Queen bee said.

Lady Marabelle led Ellie and Blue towards a large greenhouse. Once inside, Ellie observed that the fruits and vegetables grown were enormous. The first thing she saw was strawberries as big as grapefruits.

"Have a bite of one of them if you want, Ellie. I am sure you will be pleasantly surprised."

Ellie smiled and thanked Lady Marabelle. She took hold of one of the enormous strawberries and bit into it. The taste was unlike any strawberry she had ever tasted before.

"Wow, it tastes like strawberries and ice cream." Ellie wanted to eat the entire strawberry in one go.

"I wish they sold these in my local supermarket, they taste amazing," Ellie expressed, satisfied with the mouthful of strawberry she had consumed.

"Thank you, Ellie. Due to the global economic and financial crisis, I am developing new brands and hope to export them all over the world so that children in countries facing food poverty can taste the luxury of strawberries and ice cream." Ellie thought Lady Marabelle was an exceedingly kind lady with a big heart.

"This helps me finance my charity, which preserves original species from around the world. You might like to take some vanilla and cocoa pods with you when you leave. They are a lovely alternative to the sweets you buy in shops; just pop them in your mouth and suck on them until the flavour releases in your mouth," Lady Marabelle explained. She ran over to her Calabash pipe, which was wobbling around on the table.

Ellie observed the activity inside the pipe and watched as a large bubble started to emerge from it. Lady Marabelle clapped her hands together enthusiastically.

"Oh, it looks like we have another visitor. I wonder who it will be," she said as they all stared intently, waiting for the bubble to rise fully out of the pipe. It gently landed on the ground and burst in front of them, revealing Octavian.

"Lady Marabelle, pleased to see you; it's been a while. I must say, this is one of my favourite forms of travel. It's much gentler than the toboggans, which go too fast for me," Octavian said. "I have come with news of an emergency meeting taking place this evening." Octavian turned to address Ellie directly.

"I believe the Oracle gave you a gift of great importance, and I think this is the correct and best place to leave it."

Ellie felt in her pocket and pulled out the bag of seeds. Lady Marabelle leaned forward excitedly. Ellie looked at the bag of seeds, still not entirely understanding their importance, and agreed it was best to hand them over to Lady Marabelle.

"Thank you so much, Ellie. I will not let you down. There are over 1,000 different seeds here; I cannot wait to nurse and water them into full growth. There will be some amazing species here. The Oracle has travelled many realms in the multiverse, so we can only imagine what some of the seeds will be. Unfortunately, our transportation systems still limit us to our universe," explained Lady Marabelle. Ellie started to understand the importance of the small packet of seeds she had in her possession, as Lady Marabelle mused over the contents.

"I think I understand the importance of the water I drank at the 'One Thing and One Thing Only' shop. It is essential for the growth of the seeds," Ellie mused. Lady Marabelle patted Ellie on the back in recognition of her realisation.

"I do hope there is a moonflower in this bag; they are a terrific way to illuminate the house at night and, of course, excellent for the environment. They will help the world reduce its carbon footprint."

Octavian observed his watch. "We had better hurry to get to the emergency meeting," he urged.

All four of them agreed to travel via the bubble transportation system.

"Since it is Ellie's first time in the bubble, she can accompany Octavian," Lady Marabelle added.

They returned to Bluebell Cottage, where Lady Marabelle picked up an illuminous pink bottle with a simple sticker that read 'World Travel Bubbles'. Ellie watched as Lady Marabelle poured the bubble solution into the pipe. The substance was thick, pink, and stretchy. The pipe gurgled, made a spitting sound, and three large bubbles popped out of it.

12

Lady Marabelle approached the first bubble and walked into it as it sealed around her. She waved at the three remaining travel companions as her bubble took to the sky.

Blue could see Lady Marabelle waving in her bubble as she drifted off. As soon as the bubble left the grounds of the cottage, it disappeared. Blue entered his bubble, bid farewell, and he too was gone.

"Octavian, before I get in this bubble with you, is it safe? Why can't I see the other bubbles anymore? Have they just vanished?" Ellie asked, her hand tightly held by Octavian.

"It's a safe and old method of travel. Interdimensional bubble travel has been around for centuries, and no one's bubble has ever burst," Octavian reassured her, but Ellie was still unconvinced.

"I promise to keep us safe, Ellie. We need to get to the old oak tree quickly as the pods are the fastest way to get to the hall. I sense an urgency for this meeting." Ellie nodded in bewilderment.

"When we pass through the Upperworld, the bubbles will become invisible to the human eye. The public is not yet ready to handle this type of information, so it's best to keep it a secret. Alright, here we go, Ellie. Just walk slowly and gently into the bubble with me. You may feel a popping in your ears."

Ellie was in awe as she found herself floating in the skies above, invisible to the human eye, yet able to see everything. It was an incredible view, and Octavian looked comfortable as he sat down in the bubble. Ellie, feeling a bit wobbly, followed suit, and sat down beside him. The view was truly breathtaking, and as a flock of birds flew by, one of them curiously peered at them as if to ask why they were in its domain.

Ellie approached the town where she lived and could see Grandpa Jo's farm, then the old church. As they neared the entrance to the Underworld, the old oak tree came into view. Everything was going smoothly until they hit an air pocket and the bubble spiralled out of control, causing Octavian to shout.

"Don't worry, just hold on tight. We'll pass through it soon. It's just an air pocket. I should have warned you about them, but the weather looked calm. We're about to have a bumpy landing, so brace yourself," Octavian reassured Ellie as the bubble spiralled out of control.

Ellie's face and hands pressed against the side of the bubble, and while she was worried the bubble might burst, she was also relieved that no one could see how ridiculous she looked.

They quickly approached the old oak tree as Ellie braced herself for the landing. The bubble hit the ground next to the tree and bounced several times before finally bursting and disintegrating. Octavian and Ellie hit the ground with a harsh bump, sending them rolling across the ground.

Ellie winced and rubbed her sore backside. "Ouch, that hurt," she muttered, as she looked up to the sound of hearty laughter. She grabbed hold of the hand extended out to her and Kyle pulled her up, still laughing. "Kyle, it's not funny. I was so scared, I thought the bubble was going to burst in the air and smash me into the ground," Ellie grumbled, trying to straighten out her dishevelled appearance while hiding her embarrassment.

"What's so funny?" Ellie asked, not amused by Kyle's teasing.

She gave him a sharp look to match what she was feeling, which only made him laugh even harder. Just as Ellie was about to give Kyle a piece of her mind, they heard the voice of Bob Bomtane behind them.

"To the toboggan pods, we need to get to the Grand Council meeting urgently. There are some serious and distressing matters we all need to address, so HURRY," Bob announced.

The meeting started without any formalities as Bob Bomtane immediately addressed the urgent matter at hand.

"Welcome, by now you are all aware that King Jamari has switched to the other side and is now forming part of Katia's formidable army. We have been trying with every desperate effort to enter talks with the King to win his favour back. We had been making great progress in succeeding, but have now faced a terrible setback," Bob Bomtane sighed.

"A human poacher has shot and killed one of the King's cousins. As you can imagine, this has deeply saddened and angered him. Since the incident, King Jamari has been on a predatory prowl to kill the poacher to avenge the death of his cousin."

The hall was silent, with heads bowed, and a sense of understanding of King Jamari's grief could be observed on the faces of the crowd.

"This has only strengthened Katia's argument that the Underworld has been slow in their movement to deal with a defence against the atrocities, which some - and I emphasise some - humans are committing," Bob stated. The crowd, which was made up of humans, animals, and creatures from all corners of the planet, were all sympathetic to the Underworld's cause.

"The problem is, we really cannot afford for King Jamari and his clan to switch sides and become our enemy. One of the main reasons for this urgent meeting today is to use the King's descent to the other side to our advantage. Today, I request volunteers to join Katia's army to spy on them. I know this is asking a lot from our loyal followers, but we need to use deception to win the upcoming battle we all face."

As Bob Bomtane finished his speech, stunned faces of both humans and animals looked at him, and whispers began to fill the hall. It was Kyle who stood up first.

"I will do it," Kyle declared, breaking the stunned silence.

Ellie's stomach churned with worry at the thought of him getting caught. She knew that Katia was ruthless towards spies and traitors. After a few moments of gasps and whispers, Bob Bomtane turned to face Kyle.

"Most admirable of you, Kyle. You must go away and think of a good, solid story as to why you left our movement. Once you have rehearsed this story airtight, go to Katia and ask to join her army. You must learn to operate under her instruction and be prepared to fight and train with her army. I believe it is too dangerous for you to go alone. You need to take a small team from the Underworld with you. I think that if large numbers of people go with you, it will look suspicious."

Fang from the wolf clan was the next to volunteer. "I'm sick of Katia's she-wolves giving us a bad reputation. As a result, the rest of the wolf packs are being hunted with increased ferocity by humans who fear us. I can easily enter the stronghold because one of the she-wolves used to be my companion. I know she will take me back due to our previous bond," Fang explained. Bob nodded in acceptance of Fang's offer.

Jasper stood up. "You'll need a horse to accompany you so we can learn the formation of Katia's combat horses. They will be a big part of her army, and she has a massive band of 500 horses called the Black

Pioneers. I know this because I was once one of them."

A large gasp went around the hall, and some shook their heads in dismay. The Black Pioneers were notoriously lethal in combat and didn't care who they killed, attacked, or stampeded.

"I was ashamed of what I had become. I once killed a man, and I'm not proud of it. The pressure Katia puts on the Black Pioneers is unbearable. She doesn't hesitate to whip and brand them if they disobey her orders," Jasper scorned. "But I have a hidden advantage. I am a shapeshifter, and this was never disclosed to Katia."

The crowd watched as Jasper transformed into a man in his 30s with black hair tied back in a ponytail, with a white stripe running through it, the same streak that graced his mane. He then removed his shirt, revealing six wound marks an inch in thickness and the length of his back.

"This is what Katia's own hands did. So, you see, I have a good reason for wanting to volunteer."

People bowed their heads in shame after being quick to judge Jasper's involvement with the Black Pioneers. Bob Bomtane granted Jasper's wish to be a volunteer.

The next person to stand up was a woman named Carmel. The crowd gasped once again as if the shock of the volunteers was causing them anguish. However, her husband, Frannie was the first to object.

"Please sit down, Carmel. You don't want to go back to our old ways. You have left all that behind," Frannie objected.

Ellie observed Carmel, who was petite and youthful in appearance, with short, blonde elfin-style hair. Her demeanour was mouse-like, and when she spoke, you had to strain to hear her.

Instead of dismissing her, Bob offered Carmel the same chance as the others to explain what she felt she could provide on the mission.

"Carmel, what do you think you can bring to this band of volunteers, and are you sure it is a mission you want to partake in?" Bob asked.

Despite her husband's objections, Carmel stood up and began to roar so loudly that the whole room had to cover their ears. Her eyes turned red, and fangs protruded from her mouth. She closed her eyes and placed one hand on her head and the other outstretched toward Frannie. Within seconds, Frannie was motionless, his skin pale and a small amount of blood trickling from his nose.

Members of the congregation scurried from their seats and headed out of the hall, shrieking. Carmel then proceeded to place her hands on Frannie's head for several minutes until he regained consciousness and the colour in his face slowly returned. Betty Lacelett, who was sitting near Frannie, handed him a tissue to wipe his nose, and he held up his hand to pronounce he was fine.

Carmel then explained to the crowd, "My father was a demon from the depths of the Underworld, a place where no one dared to venture. He had connections to Katia, and she used his powers at her command to kill. I grew up in the Upperworld and was taught not to use my powers. I have telekinetic abilities, with the power to tap into anyone's mind and control them. And if necessary, I can telepathically shut down their brain to the point of death." Ellie wondered how this tiny woman could cause so much destruction.

Carmel continued, "I met Frannie when I was in a dark place and had started using my powers against anyone who tried to hurt me. Frannie promised never to hurt or leave me, but in return, I agreed not to use my powers again. With my full potential, I could kill someone without using my ability to bring them back to life again. These are the same powers that Katia holds. Please permit me to join the others. I am stronger than most of you can imagine and understand how Katia works and manipulates others."

Bob paced back and forth. "How do you plan to deal with Katia and convince her of your defection?" he asked.

"That part is easy, Bob. All I need to do is stage a breakup with Frannie. I will tell her that he left me, and I am bitter with him and anyone who chooses to be his friend," Carmel replied confidently.

"Frannie, what are your thoughts on this? I understand that Carmel is responsible for her path in life, and after witnessing what she is capable of, I have no doubt that she can defend herself if needed," Bob said.

Frannie bowed his head and avoided eye contact with his wife.

"Carmel can do as she wishes. This will benefit all of us," he said, nodding. Bob accepted Frannie's statement.

"I think we should take a break now. This will give you all a chance to see if you have any hidden talents that could benefit the group."

Ellie chased after Kyle as he left the hall.

"Hey, Kyle, why did you volunteer? Do you understand how dangerous this mission will be, or did you just volunteer to prove that you're not weak? This is not the time to put on a show of bravado," she said, concern etched on her face.

Kyle shrugged in response. "No, Ellie, you're wrong. This is the time for bravado, and you have no right to challenge me on this. It's for the good of all of us, and if I'm honest, you in particular. If Katia has the second strongest elemental on her side for a while, it will keep her happy," Kyle said, shrugging off Ellie's concern. Ellie felt her blood rise at Kyle's response, and even more so for his arrogance in suggesting a hierarchy of strength among the elementals.

"I stress 'for a while' because Katia will eventually get bored using my power and come looking for the elemental with the strongest powers, which happens to be you. So, I am trying to buy you time before she comes looking for you. But we need you to grow in strength first and gain confidence in what you can achieve with your powers. Octavian and Amber will continue to train you while I am gone. So, I had every reason to volunteer, Ellie."

Ellie realised Kyle was a strategist at heart and felt bad about how she had spoken to him.

"I'm sorry, Kyle. I didn't mean to insult or offend you. I was just...never mind. I wish you luck and stay safe," Ellie apologised. Kyle smiled and nodded.

"I understand your concern for me, Ellie."

Ellie walked away, knowing she wanted to plead with him to stay, but she also knew it wouldn't deter him. He was protecting her, and she was scared he might not come back alive. She couldn't bear the thought of losing another person she cared for, but she couldn't bring herself to tell him.

This was a sombre day for the Underworld. Tension could be felt all around, and the preparation for the upcoming battle had begun. Ellie realised her life would never be the same again, and the girl she was when she first arrived in the Underworld was long gone. In moments like these, she missed her mum dearly, and a tear rolled down her cheek as she longed to feel safe. She heard the familiar and loving voices of her dad and Grandpa Jo. She turned around and threw her arms around them, grateful for their presence.

"Today has been terrible, and there's just so much sad news. I don't think I can take it," Ellie said, her voice trembling with emotion.

She knew she might have to face the loss of more people she cared about, in the coming months. Unfortunately, things were about to get even worse, as her Grandpa Jo would be the next to volunteer. Nothing would stop Grandpa Jo from volunteering. Katia had never met Jo and did not know what he looked like or who he was.

"Ellie, my dear, I have something important to tell you. Please come with me to the meditation room where it will be quiet, and we can talk."

Ellie wasn't sure what to expect, but she smiled and linked her arm with his as they walked into the room. The scent of lavender filled her nostrils as she looked up at the fibre optic lighting that resembled stars on the ceiling. The room was cosy with oversized cushions on the floor, and Grandpa Jo took a seat on one and patted another cushion for Ellie to sit next to him. She sat down and he took her hand in his.

"Ellie, my beautiful granddaughter, you know you are so dear to me. I have something to tell you that you will not be happy with. I have decided to go on this mission. I must go. It is important to me that Katia never gets to take the life of someone I love again. So, before we go back to the hall, I am asking for your blessing."

Ellie held her head in her hands, sobbing. She knew in her heart she did not want Grandpa Jo to go, but in her head, she knew he needed to go. Ellie turned to Grandpa Jo and squeezed his hand.

"Grandpa, you know I love you, and you have my blessing. I know you need to do this. I will be brave for you. I don't mean to be rude, but what hidden powers do you have to offer the mission?" Ellie asked.

Grandpa Jo chuckled in response. "You will be surprised, and I must add that you will see my skills in the hall. Don't worry, I will not let you down, and I will come back alive," he replied.

There was a knock on the door, and a voice from the other side informed Ellie and her grandpa that it was time to return to the hall.

"Come on, Ellie, we will be strong together in this battle. Let us make our way back to the hall."

13

The mood in the grand hall had changed, and faces were full of anxiety. Bob Bomtane looked dishevelled as he approached the rostrum to address the waiting audience.

"Alright, let's get back to business. We still need more volunteers. I'm sure you've all had a chance to think and discuss whether you should volunteer. Remember, your reason for leaving here will need to be solid to convince Katia and her followers that you genuinely want to join her army."

There was movement at the back of the hall. A hooded figure stood up, removed her hood and revealed a young Amber.

"No, Amber, the council will not allow you to go, no matter how much of a benefit you would be to the group. We cannot afford to have two elementals going on this mission. Please sit down. I do appreciate your concern." Amber stormed out of the hall, looking upset and defiant in her decision to volunteer.

Ellie felt nervous. She knew Grandpa Jo was the next to volunteer, and the Grand Council would not turn him down. Bob gestured for Jo to stand.

"May I address the Grand Council? As you are all aware, Katia and her she-wolves murdered my one and only daughter. The next closest thing to me is Ellie, my dearest granddaughter. I made a vow to myself to honour and avenge my daughter's death, and to protect my granddaughter at all times." There was a sombre look on people's faces.

"I have no choice. I have spoken to Ellie in private and have her blessing. Many of you may be wondering how this older man in front of you can fight. Please do not be deceived by what you see. In my younger years, many people referred to me as the Master Archer. Bill, please pass me my bow and arrows. What you cannot see, is at the back of the hall on the wall is a small X, marked there earlier by Bob Bomtane." Bill passed the bow and quiver with the arrows snugly placed inside, to Jo.

"I will show you my precision. I never miss my target. I am a hunter of all that is evil, and all that hides in the dark. They cannot escape my arrow." Grandpa Jo positioned his traditional longbow and started drawing it back to projectile the arrow to the back of the hall. The wooden arrow hardly made a sound on its trajectory through the air; it glided naturally. A sharp thud from the arrow's metal tip sounded as it hit its intended target. Stunned gasps and clapping echoed throughout the hall at the skill displayed by Grandpa Jo.

One of the spectators at the back shouted, "Direct hit."

Jo proceeded to retrieve his arrow from where it protruded out of the wall.

"Well done, Jo. An excellent job," Bob said. "As we know, Katia is recruiting men to join her deadly sharpshooters' section of the army. You do not need much of a story to enter the sharpshooters. All you need is to turn up with your bow and arrow and show your skill in their target practice. The person you need to report to on arriving at Katia's stronghold is Zeena. She oversees the deadly marksmen and is a dedicated warrior."

"Thank you, Bob and the Grand Council for your support."

The next person to stand up was Ravena, a woman in her mid-20s with short feathered black hair with a purple tint. Ravena had sharp facial features with high cheekbones and a long straight nose. Her eyes were black and beady in appearance, and it was difficult to focus on her face as she moved her head continuously in a bird-like manner.

"I would like to volunteer. As most of you know, I can shapeshift into a raven. I plan to follow the group but not join them. You will need a spy to quickly report back to the Underworld if the group of imposters you are sending gets caught. In case this happens, I can fly back to you and inform you of what has occurred. It will be easy for me to blend into the area where Katia and her followers are residing, as it is a well-known habitat for ravens." Bob carefully considered Ravena's proposal and agreed with it.

"Ravena, I like this idea, but for how long can you maintain your raven form?"

"I can remain in my raven form for up to three months without needing to shift back to human form. This will provide us with sufficient time to gather all the necessary information on Katia's upcoming attack plans."

"It is granted, Ravena. You can join the mission," Bob Bomtane said with a smile as he authorised her participation. He was beginning to feel pleased with the growing group of volunteers.

There was a lot of commotion and movement at the back of the hall as the next volunteer tried to squeeze his way through the crowd to the front. He was a cumbersome figure, standing seven feet tall and weighing 20 stone of pure muscle. Known to all who met him as Bouncing Bartholomew, and to those who loved him as the gentle giant, he was an impressive sight once he reached the front. Bartholomew's tanned, muscular body and clean-shaven skin were a testament to how much he cared for himself. As he spoke, his deep voice boomed throughout the hall.

"Bob Bomtane, it is my pleasure to offer my services to the Underworld," boomed Bartholomew in his deep voice. "I have an identical twin named Bernard, and we have worked well together in the past as bouncers. We were a formidable pair, working in local bars and clubs, and no criminal gang ever outsmarted us. The towns were safe from criminals, and any bad characters when Bernard and I worked the doors." Bartholomew looked down at the ground, a pained expression crossing his face as he recalled what he needed to say.

"Work always came our way. We had a successful business and a steady income until one day we received a job proposal from Katia's corporation to work as bouncers and act as her main security guards. It was a tempting proposition with triple our usual salary," Bartholomew paused to gather his composure to carry on.

"The offer to work for Katia was the first time Bernard and I had ever fallen out with each other. I had heard about the terrible atrocities that were happening at the hands of Katia and her corporation, so I refused the offer at all costs. Unfortunately, this did not stop Bernard, and when Katia found out about our disagreement, she offered Bernard even more money to work for her. With Bernard's departure, I have never felt complete. I know that in the last five years, he has worked for Katia and taken a wife from within the corporation. They have a baby due this week."

Bob Bomtane realised it was not easy for Bartholomew to share his private life, so he listened attentively to what he had to say. "Please continue, Bartholomew; we appreciate your honesty and depth at this time."

"Our mother has informed me that Bernard will be on leave for several months to be with his wife and the new baby in her hometown in Alaska. During this time, Bernard has asked for no communication to have time to bond fully with his child. I know his wishes will be respected, and no one would dare go against his word, except for me. I plan to impersonate my brother and return to Katia's corporation during those months when he is on leave." Bartholomew pensively paced up and down.

"I will tell them that my wife instructed me to return due to having low income, and she desires many new items for our newborn. I will stress that she finds me an annoyance being idly in her way. No one will question Bernard, so my plan is safe. Bob, if you would like, after the meeting has ended, we can all go to the Underworld's recreation area. I can then give a demonstration of my skills. The space in here is limited." Bob instructed several of the Grand Council members to prepare the recreation area for Bartholomew's demonstration.

Bob Bomtane personally introduced the next speaker to take the stand.

"May I welcome you all to the main reason we are here today on this melancholy evening. This is the lady who has organised this meeting and proposal and will also be heading the group of volunteers leaving for this dangerous quest. Please welcome Queen Jamillia, wife of Jamari."

A loud rumble of clapping and cheering erupted around the hall, and humans and animals stood up to welcome the Queen.

The Queen gracefully approached the podium and extended a warm welcome to everyone.

"Welcome and thank you for your presence and unwavering support for my husband, the King. As Bob has already mentioned, I will be leading the perilous mission ahead of us. It has been a time of great sorrow for our family since the tragic loss of the King's cousin. As you all know, the King and I have been blessed with a new addition to our family, our baby, Zion. It is a grievous matter that the King cannot be present to witness his son's growth, as he has chosen to serve under the notorious organisation of Katia." Ellie looked sad that the King would choose Katia over his son.

"Nevertheless, I am determined to retrieve my missing loved one and bring him home, where he belongs." The Queen graciously acknowledged the audience's nods of approval.

"As a queen and a mother, this is not what I want for my son or our kingdom. I have to go on this mission and deceive Katia into thinking that I am a loyal queen to my husband and that I am there to support his decision." Queen Jamillia stood tall and confident.

"I am keen to start the mission, but the truth is, I do not support my husband's wrongful actions. I am desperate to reason with him for his return to the Underworld, so we can all start to work on a new strategy in fighting the battle ahead we face. The King's way is not my way, and I know all who go on this journey are risking their lives, but we cannot sit back and do nothing and endanger ourselves." Ellie admired the choices the volunteers for the mission made.

"We must work swiftly to resolve this terrible situation. We only have three days to train and perfect our stories for this mission, then we will leave on the third night as darkness falls. I have placed my little cub, Zion in safe hands, and his whereabouts are only to be known to a trusted few." Queen Jamillia bowed her head in sadness.

"If anything goes wrong and I do not return, I trust he will be trained and made into the new king. Should this happen, please tell Zion I was a good queen, and his father was also a good king but lost his way through his disillusionment and grief. I ask one more thing before we move to the recreation area to watch Bartholomew's demonstration, and that is for Kyle to return to the stand."

Kyle looked uneasy as he returned, bowing his head as he faced the Queen and waited for her to speak.

"Thank you, mighty warrior Kyle," Queen Jamillia began. "I will be glad to have your service on this mission. However, before we embark, I need you to convince us of your reason for leaving the Underworld. What explanation will you give to Katia for your departure?" Kyle's confusion was evident.

"Kyle, you have grown up here in the Underworld, and Katia knows of your deep loyalty towards your caregivers. I need you to clearly explain your story, as yours needs to be stronger than most of the other volunteers. It will need to be grounded in some truth, so it is not exposed as a lie by Katia, or all our covers may be blown."

Kyle felt a sense of dread; he knew he had to make his reasons to Katia solid to avoid arousing her suspicions. He struggled with the concept of the story he had planned to tell her, as it involved portraying anger towards Ellie. His voice wavered as he began to speak, and he coughed to clear his throat, attempting to conceal the nerves he felt.

"Thank you, Queen Jamillia, for giving me the chance to explain. I believe I can provide you all with a solid story. I am confident I can persuade Katia of my reasons for leaving the Underworld." Kyle turned towards Ellie as he continued with his explanation.

"Most of you know that the Underworld is the only home I have ever known. When I was born, my mother left me with the Underworld, wrapped in a blanket with the initials K. P on it. There was a note that read 'I love you. I will return for you'. I was the first elemental to turn up in the Underworld, and by the time I was five, my powers were already observable.

The Underworld was amazed; they had never seen anyone like me before, with the ability to control the wind. I felt important, wanted, and very much in control." Kyle felt uncomfortable being so open with the congregation.

"Octavian was the next elemental to turn up with his unique ability to control water, followed by young Amber with her amazing work with the earth element. You see, I could deal with Octavian and Amber; they were new to their gift and had not fully developed it. But then Ellie turned up." Kyle's eyes seemed to penetrate straight into Ellie's gaze as if he were genuinely angry by her presence.

"For the first time with Ellie, I felt like I had competition. All I had heard were rumours that she was the strongest elemental out of us and that her power alone was stronger than all three of our gifts put together. Can you imagine how I felt? I wasn't the strongest anymore and I wasn't as important as Ellie. I can tell you, it's not a good feeling at all. Therefore, Queen Jamillia, I will tell Katia there's someone in the Underworld stronger than I am, and I don't like it. I will tell her that the Underworld favours this newcomer more than me. I will inform her that the one they call Ellie is the element of fire."

The hall was deadly silent when Kyle finished speaking, his words resonating with the congregation. Ellie looked dismayed by what he had said.

"Kyle, I am sorry if my presence here is making you feel insecure. I did not mean to make anyone feel pushed out, and I am certainly not better than anyone." However, Kyle did not seem to take her words seriously and broke out into laughter.

"Gotcha! This isn't how I feel, although I must commend myself on an outstanding performance. However, I do need to point out some truth in what I said. We need to do this so Katia knows about you and knows the fourth element is here. Once she knows, she will try to capture all of us to use for her benefit. So, you see, I can convince Katia, and what's more, I can take an important message to her that the fourth element is here." Bob Bomtane made his way back to the stand.

"Your permission to leave is still granted. Thank you for further clarifying the story you will use. Well, I think it's time to close the meeting and for all of us to make our way to the recreation area to watch Bartholomew's demonstration. Once again, thank you, everyone, for coming on such short notice."

The recreation area was filled with members of the congregation from the hall, all of them standing and waiting curiously. Bartholomew stepped out and instructed the crowd to form orderly lines with a gulley down the middle. The crowd obliged, and Bartholomew positioned himself at one end of the recreation area. They watched as he stood tall and took deep breaths in and out. Then, he curled himself up into a ball shape and began to spin around so quickly that he became invisible.

Suddenly, the ball that was Bartholomew accelerated to 100 miles per hour down the gully the crowd had formed. There was a wall at the other end, and the crowd watched with worry as it appeared Bartholomew would crash into the wall. But he stopped abruptly, just in time. The crowd gasped and breathed sighs of relief. Bartholomew stood up once again, bowing to their cheers.

"I must emphasise that if needed, I could have smashed straight through the wall, but I did not think the council would appreciate the cost and labour of having to rebuild it. For my next demonstration, I need two good-sized volunteers. This is just to show you a sample of my strength. As you can see, I have had to limit what I can do so that nobody gets hurt and nothing is broken. The true reality is I can do a lot more than what I am showing you today." Two men who were over six feet and 16 stone each stepped forward.

Bartholomew instructed the men to stand on either side of him and then proceeded to pick them up under each arm, lifting them in the air simultaneously. The men looked bewildered as they were held up in the air. Despite their concern, the crowd cheered and whistled as Bartholomew displayed his incredible strength. He then placed the men back on the ground, thanked them for participating, turned to the crowd, and took a bow.

As the crowd struggled to regain their composure after Bartholomew's incredible performance, a gust of wind appeared out of nowhere, creating a small cyclone with a vortex at its centre in the middle of the recreation area. People held onto each other to avoid being pulled into the vortex, and various objects were sucked into it, including hats, glasses, bits of paper, and even someone's wig. Then, just as suddenly as it started, the wind stopped, and Kyle emerged from the spot where the cyclone had been.

"I apologise for not warning you, but I thought it was only fair to give a mini demonstration of my powers while I had the opportunity. If anyone lost any valuables during the demonstration, I have them all here. If anything is damaged, I will replace it. Thank you." The man who had lost his wig hastily retrieved it.

Bob Bomtane took centre stage in the recreation area and chuckled. "Don't worry, I don't have any fancy demonstrations to share with you. I just want to wish you all a safe journey home and say a big thank you to everyone. The volunteers will be leaving from here in three nights if you wish to say goodbye to them." The crowd dispersed, chatting amongst themselves as they left. Ellie reunited with Grandpa Jo and her dad.

"I think it's time to call it a night."

Ellie and Bill nodded. Grandpa Jo and the volunteers would need all the rest they could get before heading off into the Forbidden Underworld.

14

The eight volunteers sat in one of the available classrooms in the Underworld, each with a printout. Bob Bomtane stood in front of the interactive whiteboard, looking serious. Carmel stifled a laugh as she noticed Bob's glasses perched on the end of his nose.

Queen Jamillia and Fang reclined on a luxurious purple padded cover, enjoying the comfort before their journey. The rest of the volunteers were seated on chairs made from reclaimed wood, carved with intricate designs, and adorned with green plush velvet cushions. However, Bartholomew required a specially made chair brought in from the hall due to his size, as he was too large for the standard chairs.

"Alright, let's begin with the checklist. Each of you will need to have the following items:

Compass
Sleeping bag
Warm clothes
Torches and matches
Food
Water purification tablets

You may each choose one extra item to take with you, something you think will be helpful for the journey. Remember, you are fortunate to have Jasper and Bartholomew to carry your load," Bob said as he tapped the screen to change the page.

The next header read '*Journey Route*'. Bob Bomtane sat in front of the travellers, his face stern as he tapped his claws on the desk.

"Now, on to the more serious matters. Ravena, please come and finish the reading for me. My eyesight is poor, and I do not care for wearing glasses." Ravena made her way to the front of the classroom, her birdlike movements evident as she looked around from side to side.

"Entrance to the Forbidden Underworld is the first port of call. Make your way to the underground caverns and find the large stone gateway. The gateway is a portal between our Underworld and the Forbidden Underworld. How this gateway opens will be the first mystery," Ravena read aloud from the printout, her voice clear and steady.

"Your handouts give a brief outline of the stages of the journey you will encounter. Read them to familiarise yourself with what to expect." The group looked perplexed at what the journey would entail.

"If you manage the journey, then the hard part will begin. You will have to become outstanding actors to fool Katia."

"Thanks, Ravena, for reading. I think it's time for a break, and we will resume in an hour," Bob said.

The volunteers nodded in agreement, and exchanged anxious glances as they contemplated the challenges ahead. It was clear that the real test was yet to come.

**

Ellie sat at home, gazing out of the same window where she had first encountered Octavian. She wrapped her fleece blanket around her, lost in thought about what her future held. The door opened, and Grandpa Jo popped in, having snuck back from his briefing at the Underworld.

"Is there room for one more on the settee?"

Ellie smiled and patted the seat next to her. "Of course, Grandpa. Come and sit next to me." He made his way over to Ellie, clutching a shiny object in his hand. He let out a big sigh and sat down.

"I have a gift for you, or rather, a gift to share with me," Grandpa Jo said with a smile. "Remember when I mentioned that I was working on a new tracking device for you after the incident with the amulet? Well, it's finished. I think you'll like it."

Ellie looked down at his hands and saw he was holding a compact mirror. "How does it work?"

Grandpa Jo opened the compact to reveal two identical mirrors on each side. He unsnapped a locking mechanism holding the two halves together. He handed Ellie one half and kept the other half for himself.

"As you're not in school at the moment, I figured I could make a device that you can use anytime. Go ahead, look through it."

While Ellie looked through her mirror, Grandpa Jo looked through his. She couldn't help but laugh as she saw in the mirror the image of him sticking his tongue out at her. At the same time, his mirror showed Ellie laughing back at him.

"You're a genius; this is so cool!" Ellie exclaimed, her eyes filled with wonder.

Grandpa Jo looked visibly pleased and grateful. "All those years of mad solitude in my shed have served me well," he chuckled.

"On this journey, I can take one personal item, and I've decided to take my half of the mirror, so we'll never be apart from each other. I can track your safety, and you can track me. I've put a little switch on it, so if we need privacy, we can just press it."

Ellie observed the button on the mirror. "What's next to the button?"

Grandpa Jo spoke into the mirror, and Ellie could hear his voice.

"Yours is the same too. We can use it to communicate with each other."

As the moon shone through the window, it cast its grandeur and magnitude into the room. Grandpa Jo stared at it; it would be a long time before he would see that sight again. Where he was going, there would be no moon or sun, nothing to distinguish day from night. Ellie looked at her grandpa's face and could see the anxiety in his eyes. Even though she would be able to see him through her mirror, she knew it wouldn't be the same as being with him in person.

"It's getting late now; I'm afraid I've missed the second half of my briefing at the Underworld. I'm sure one of the other volunteers will fill me in on what I've missed. I need to go to bed and rest. My dear Ellie, you must train and strengthen your gift for when Katia and her followers come looking for you."

Ellie gave him a big hug, feeling a mixture of gratitude and worry. "Goodnight, Grandpa. I love you."

"I love you too."

***

Ellie awoke on the day the travellers were due to leave and glanced at her clock; she had been so tired that she hadn't even heard the cockerel crow. The walk downstairs felt like an eternity. When she reached the bottom of the stairs, she saw all of Grandpa Jo's packed items for his journey. His bow and arrows were in carrying cases, standing upright next to his bags. She found him in the garden with her dad, practising his aim with his spare bow set.

"Ellie, will you accompany Grandpa Jo to the Underworld?"

"I'd love to," she replied, smiling at her dad.

Ellie kicked the fallen leaves from the trees on the ground and smiled. It would bring her pleasure to accompany Grandpa Jo. She could also say goodbye to Kyle and wish him well before he set off.

"It's time to go now, Grandpa."

A hand touched Ellie's shoulder, she jumped; it was Kyle.

"Oh, you startled me. You have a way of always making me jump." Ellie smiled; she was growing fond of him.

"Come on, Jo. I will help you carry your bags; I thought you both would appreciate me coming to escort you."

The threesome set off toward the old oak tree in silence. Grandpa Jo clutched his bow and arrow as if his life depended on it.

They had too many bags to travel in the toboggan pods; instead, they used the entrance via the hidden trap door. The stairway down into the Underworld was lit by the fireflies, giving it a lovely warm glow. They came to an arched wooden door. Kyle pulled out a large gold key and opened it. Once they were all through the door, he was careful to lock it behind them as they entered the familiar territory of the Underworld. They walked up the corridor toward the meeting room where the other travellers were waiting for them. The group huddled together, chatting by the open fire to get every bit of warmth to their bodies before setting off on their journey.

Carmel greeted them and seemed in high spirits.

"Good evening, grab a drink. Apart from you, Ellie. It is only meant for those going on the journey. It is the item I chose to bring with me, I did not brew any extra."

Ellie observed the small glasses of orange coloured drink the travellers were sipping. There were two glasses left on the table, one for Grandpa Jo and one for Kyle.

"The drink will enable us to keep warm for up to three months. That way we will not need to light fires in the Forbidden Underworld. This will help us, especially in the dragon's den, as they are attracted to fire. They may attack us if they see the fire is not from their natural breath." Ellie thought the journey they were going on sounded dangerous but at the same time an adventure she would have liked to embark on.

Blue announced to Jo that he would be accompanying them on their journey to the stone entrance, due to his tracking skills.

"Although I am coming with you, I will be departing at the entrance to Katia's town and returning to the Underworld." The decision for Blue to accompany them had been Ravena's idea. He had been the one thing she had chosen to bring, even if it was only for part of the journey.

"I had a dream that Blue would be able to help us gain access to the Forbidden Underworld through the stone gate," Ravena explained.

There was no time for the other group members to discuss the items they had brought, as time was pressing for them to leave the Underworld. It was also time for the shapeshifters to assume the desired form they would be travelling in.

15

It was unanimously agreed that Jasper would travel in his horse form, so he could be saddled and carry the bags of the travellers. Jasper could provide respite for the group, and if weary, they could ride upon him. Ravena chose to take her raven form so she could, as planned, fly ahead, and look out for impending danger.

It was safe territory for Ravena due to the Forbidden Underworld being the home of the ravens. The ravens in this territory were known to be an antisocial bunch, so there was no need for her to mix and risk blowing her cover. It was agreed that Ravena would be the only member to leave the group. Fang would adopt his wolf identity to take over tracking when Blue would depart from the group.

The rest of the group stayed in their respective forms but maintained a specific formation, with Ravena leading the way and often flying ahead. Next in line were the two trackers, Fang and Blue. Carmel followed closely behind, being half-demon and feeling no fear in the Forbidden Underworld. Her demon abilities would make her a formidable opponent in any battle they might face. Jo followed with his exceptional archery skills, ready to unleash his deadly arrows if needed.

Jasper was positioned next in the group, with Queen Jamillia by his side. Both Jasper and the

Queen required top-notch protection, not because they were weak, but because they held significant importance. Jasper was a valuable means of transportation, while the Queen served as a tactical asset in winning back the loyalty of King Jamari. The Queen possessed many strengths, including deadly fighting skills and remarkable speed. Her tracking abilities to locate enemies were honed to the highest degree.

Poor Bartholomew was positioned at the back of the group for several reasons, primarily due to his size which slowed him down. However, Bartholomew being at the rear also had its advantages as he could serve as a lookout, protecting the group from any potential attacks coming from behind.

The group bid Ellie a heartfelt farewell, and Grandpa Jo gave her a big hug.

"Don't forget to use your mirror, Ellie. I wish you great success with your training," he said.

The rest of the group took turns hugging her as well. Overwhelmed with emotions, Ellie turned away from the group, finding it too difficult to watch them leave, especially her beloved grandpa. Blue led the group out of the meeting room.

***

"Follow me, this way. It will be essential for the last one out of the door to make sure it is securely locked behind us," Blue said, leading the group down a corridor towards a large, heavily padlocked steel door.

A plaque above it read, '*The Caverns to the Forbidden Underworld.*' Earlier, Bob Bomtane had given Blue the keys with strict instructions to lock the door behind them. It took both Blue and Kyle to open the heavy door. Kyle sensed the trepidation ahead of them.

The door creaked loudly as it was opened. It had only been opened on three occasions before. The smell of dampness and earth invaded the travellers' noses. Freezing air circulated them as they entered. Kyle observed Carmel as she took a deep breath and wrapped her coat around her.

"Are you cold, Carmel?"

"Trust me, if we hadn't drunk the special elixir, the air would have been too cold for some of us to enter. The elixir will work stronger in an hour, so we will get warmer. For now, stay close. Our body heat will help keep us warm," Carmel explained. The heavy door slammed loudly behind them, causing the group of travellers to jump.

"Scary," Bartholomew muttered, though given his size, one would have thought he wouldn't spook easily.

The atmosphere in the Forbidden Underworld corridor was foreboding. Jasper snorted as if angered by the noise of the door. Carmel turned around and stroked his mane to calm him. Blue quickly padlocked the door to prevent any unknown entities from escaping into the Underworld, or worse, into the Upperworld.

The corridor leading to the stone gateway was narrow and low in height, requiring Bartholomew to squeeze through and bend down.

"Blimey, I would be better off crawling," Bartholomew grumbled.

Nobody in the group seemed to mind his complaints, as the environment they were in was far from pleasant, a stark contrast to the bright corridors of the Underworld to which they were accustomed. Kyle stumbled; the ground underneath them was uneven, with large twigs and stones scattered everywhere.

"I'm sure I've been here before. The smell and chilly air are giving me flashbacks of an old memory, but I can't make sense of it," Kyle said, furrowing his brow and feeling confused.

Fang, who was sniffing the ground below, looked up at Kyle with a questioning expression. "I too have a very distant smell of your scent that I am picking up," Fang said, his senses heightened as he continued to sniff the ground.

"I don't know why, as far as I can remember I haven't been here before," Kyle replied, puzzled by the faint memories. The group exchanged curious glances, but there was no time to dwell on it as they had to press on through the narrow, uneven corridor towards the stone gateway in the Forbidden Underworld.

"I think we need more lighting in here," Jo said, reaching into his pocket and turning on his hand-cranked torch.

Solar torches would be ineffective where they were going, as there would be no sunlight for the duration of their journey into the Forbidden Underworld. The torch provided more than adequate lighting, illuminating their path through the dark and foreboding corridor. Kyle was feeling glad for the light and his resourceful companions.

Several metres ahead of the group, the tunnel expanded and grew lighter.

"Bartholomew, you will be glad to know that we are now near the end of the narrow tunnel," Blue said, casting a reassuring glance.

Bartholomew grunted and looked extremely uncomfortable as he squeezed through the narrow passage. "Good, the corridor made me feel claustrophobic," he replied, taking a deep breath as he emerged from the tunnel.

The group found themselves in a large cavern with three entrances in front of them. Bartholomew straightened his back, and it emitted a terrible cracking sound. Kyle gave him a worrying glance.

"No worries, just straightening my bones out," Bartholomew chuckled.

Ravena materialised at their side in her human form. "Which way now, Blue?" Ravena asked, looking at him with curiosity.

"There is only one entrance; the other two entrances are illusions that lead to dead ends. I know how to figure this out. Fang, this is where I need your help," Blue explained confidently.

Fang proudly walked forward to stand next to Blue, his fur immaculately full and groomed to a high standard, making him a truly handsome wolf to look at. Blue crouched down to Fang's level, ready to communicate with him. Kyle waited eagerly.

"Fang, I need you to howl into each entrance. We need to see how far your howl will carry and how quickly the echo returns to us. This will tell us which the correct entrance is. The true entrance is a long distance," Blue instructed.

Fang nodded, understanding his role in determining the correct entrance to the Forbidden Underworld. He took a step back, positioning himself in front of the entrances, and let out a long, resonant howl that echoed throughout the cavern. The group waited in anticipation, listening for the echoes to return, and observing how far Fang's howl carried into each entrance.

"This is easy for me to judge. I knew as soon as I approached the second entrance. The howl had taken the longest to return after it travelled its many twists and turns," Fang reported to the group with certainty.

Blue nodded in agreement, trusting Fang's keen senses and instincts. It was clear that the second entrance was the correct path to take. Kyle looked on with gratitude.

As the travellers entered the cave, a pungent sulphur smell greeted their senses and Kyle held his hand over his nose.

"If anyone wants to turn back, this is your last chance. Now is the time to speak up if anyone is not happy with continuing on this journey," Blue stated, looking around at the group.

The silence that followed did not necessarily indicate unanimous agreement, but rather a shared determination to fight for the cause. There was an element of bravado emanating from each of the travellers, but deep down inside, Kyle couldn't help but feel scared of what lay ahead.

They had been walking for miles in the caves without encountering any signs of life, not even a cave bat; until ahead of them, they heard fresh running water and the faint voices of children singing and laughing. Carmel, who had been quiet for a while, looked astonished.

"Why are there children down here? This is not a place for children to be in," Carmel exclaimed.

The group turned the corner and gasped. In the middle of the cave was a beautiful, cascading waterfall. At the edges of the cave was a sandy beach, it looked like a tropical island.

Everywhere the travellers looked, children could be seen building sandcastles, swimming, and playing ball games, and engaging in all sorts of activities one would expect to find on a beach.

Bartholomew scratched his head in confusion. "This is not what I had prepared for," he murmured. Some of the children stopped and stared at the group as they entered the cave. Bartholomew observed the children with a perplexed expression on his face.

"They look no different from the children of the Upperworld," Bartholomew stated. On closer inspection, the first child they encountered had violet-coloured eyes, while another had yellow eyes, and yet another had pink.

"Demon children," Carmel whispered, noting the unique eye colours. She was half-demon herself. "I mean no insult."

"Hey, where are you going?" shouted one of the children, while another child also addressed the group.

"If you continue straight up there, you'll end up at the dragon's den. I wouldn't go there if I were you," the child advised. "Dragons don't like visitors. Our parents tell us never to go there."

"We have no choice; we are going to join Katia's army," declared Kyle.

One by one, the children turned their backs on the travellers. "We have been brought up not to mix with anybody from Katia's army. Our parents have told us that Katia and her followers are a bad lot. They want us to leave the Forbidden Underworld and live in the

Underworld for our protection, even though we are demons."

Queen Jamillia addressed the children's concerns, "We mean you no harm; we will pass on through and be out of your way. Please be at ease." The group continued their way, knowing that the dragon's den was their next stop.

16

The travellers pressed on towards their next destination. After 10 minutes of walking, they arrived at the entrance of a new cave, and Kyle heard the sound of roaring flames. Ravena, who was flying ahead, soared higher to get a view of how many dragons were inside. She squawked, signalling her findings to the group.

"It's not good. They are everywhere, some big and some small," Ravena reported. "The dragons are randomly breathing out flames." Kyle was almost looking forward to seeing a dragon, he had never seen one.

"Fire is a big fear of mine," Jasper said, shaking his mane and flaring his nostrils.

"If it helps to keep you calm, I will ride upon your back," Jo offered.

"Thank you. It may just help me," Jasper replied gratefully.

The group slowly made their way into the cave, remembering what they had learnt before setting off - that dragons will only attack if they feel threatened. Kyle gasped with amazement. There were dragons of every type and in a vast array of colours in the cave. Dragons climbed the walls, flew past them, and some lay on the rocks sleeping. Bartholomew spotted several dragonesses nesting their unborn in their eggs, while some were nursing their newborns.

"Best to stay away from the nursing mothers, they may think you have come for their young or their eggs. The eggs are sold at the illegal markets, at Katia's stronghold."

Kyle was taken aback by Bartholomew's statement. "How wrong to take the babies away from their mothers."

The journey through the den was going safely until a dragon jumped in front of the group. Fang snarled at the dragon who was staring right at him.

"At ease, Fang. Remember, show no danger. I know your instinct may be to attack and fight, but you will be no match for the dragon's fiery breath," cautioned Bartholomew.

The dragon, not much bigger than Fang, circled him with entrails of smoke wisping out of its breath. More dragons had lined the path on either side of the travellers. Bartholomew reached inside his pocket and pulled out a long silver whistle, blowing it loudly. Kyle watched in amusement as Bartholomew's cheeks puffed out.

The travellers themselves could not hear the sound emanating from the whistle, but the dragons could. Some of the dragons shrieked in response to the high-pitched noise and retreated from the group.

"Bartholomew, what is it you have?" Jo looked intrigued.

"It's a dragon whistle, given to me when I was a small boy by my mother; she told me one day I would need this. I didn't understand why, I do now."

The remainder of the dragons had backed away to the recesses of the cave as they waited for the group to pass through. Now, they were free to continue their journey, but they knew that more dangers lay ahead.

"That wasn't too bad." Kyle sat down to rest on a rock, feeling relieved but also grateful for having seen the magnificent creatures.

"Our next encounter is with the Rock Men, so as long as we stay away from the walls where they dwell, we should be fine," Bartholomew said.

"I don't fancy being grabbed by some large man made of stone; I'm in no way strong enough to get away from their grip," Kyle scoffed.

"I'm quite looking forward to an encounter with them. It's just my kind of thing, bring it on, Rock Men. Just because they think they are rock solid does not mean they can defeat me," Bartholomew said with enthusiasm. The rest of the group was amused by his light-hearted humour, amid their journey, and welcomed the moment.

"Right, come on, I am ready for those Rock Men, let's go," Bartholomew exclaimed, flexing his muscles in anticipation of the challenge.

Ravena did her sweeping fly in and out to check the next cave before they entered. "I cannot see a soul, nothing at all."

Jo shook his head. "Oh, they will be there, sneaky blighters. I have been told they are masters of camouflage," Jo warned as the group set off into the cave.

Ravena was correct, there was no one in sight. Kyle made sure he stayed in the middle of the path and kept a vigilant eye on the walls on either side of him.

"What was that? I'm sure I just saw something move. It looked like an eyeball," Kyle said, pointing to a part of the wall.

Blue squatted down on the ground and observed some large footprints. He then placed his ear to the ground, listening intently.

"There is someone in here. I can hear muffled talking from somewhere in the cave," Blue alerted the group.

Up ahead, there was a narrower part of the cave, which wouldn't be an issue for most of the travellers. However, it would be a tight squeeze for Bartholomew, making it challenging for him to avoid touching the sides of the walls.

"Jo, I'm not sure I can fit through as a horse. I am going to shift back to my human form," Jasper said. Jo climbed off Jasper's back.

They started to walk through the narrow tunnel, with Bartholomew walking sideways to give himself some wiggle room. Kyle couldn't help feeling sorry for the struggle Bartholomew was having.

The floor beneath them was slippery from the water cascading down the walls, making the moss on the path beneath them slimy. There was an almighty bang as Bartholomew slipped. Jo shone his torch on the walls, and about 20 pairs of eyes opened. Bartholomew tried his best to stand up as he observed the figures that had started to move in the surrounding walls. Kyle knew they were in trouble.

"Run!" Bartholomew yelled to the others.

"I don't like the idea of leaving you. I am staying with you. If I switch back to horse form, I can help by stampeding some of the Rock Men," Jasper said determinedly.

The rest of the group ran off ahead, ushered by Kyle and made their way out of the Rock Men's cave, leaving Jasper and Bartholomew to face the impending battle. They could only wait in anticipation and hope for their companion's victory. There were now at least 20 Rock Men gathered in the narrow tunnel.

"You're mine!" shouted Bartholomew, running at a group of five Rock Men and sending them toppling like skittles; he was triumphant in his glory. They lay in a heap, now a big pile of rubble. Further up the tunnel, Jasper reared on his hind legs and lunged forward at one of the Rock Men, creating a loud crashing sound that echoed outside the cave.

"Hey, Jasper, they may be big and strong, but the saying 'the bigger they are, the harder they fall' is true," Bartholomew called out with a grin, as he continued to fend off the Rock Men with his formidable strength, loving every moment of the challenge.

One of the Rock Men charged at Bartholomew, and with a swift punch, he sent it tumbling to the ground. Meanwhile, a large group of over 50 Rock Men formed at the tunnel exit. Bartholomew quickly came up with a plan and knew in his heart he could defeat them.

"Jasper, I have a plan. I will use my bouncing and rolling ball technique. When I smash into them, you charge at full speed through them. This should give us the chance to get out of here," Bartholomew surmised.

"Good plan, Bartholomew. Let's put it into practice," Jasper said, nodding in agreement.

The odd-looking pair walked back up to the beginning of the narrow tunnel entrance. The Rock Men could be heard mumbling to each other, clearly confused about what the two travellers were doing.

Bartholomew stopped walking and started to take deep breaths, and then curled up into a ball, just as he had done during the demonstration in the grand hall. He started spinning and bouncing along the narrow tunnel at a breakneck pace. As he approached the group of Rock Men, he accelerated his speed, bouncing and smashing into the large group. Jasper waited, ready to spring into action as soon as Bartholomew gave him the signal.

"Go now, Jasper!" Bartholomew called out.

Upon hearing the signal, Jasper charged forward at full speed. Some of the Rock Men managed to jump back into the security of their wall, remaining silent, the rest were trampled into piles of rubble by Jasper's stampede. Dust filled the narrow tunnel and billowed out of the cave exit.

"Oh, my goodness, do you think they're okay?" cried Ravena.

As the dust began to settle, two shadowy figures walked out of the cave. It was Bartholomew and Jasper. Cries of celebration erupted from the group of travellers. Although Bartholomew was pleased with the result, he was relieved he would live to see another day.

***

"Is everyone hungry?" Jo asked, and a unanimous grunt came from the group.

Jo decided it was time to eat and rest before the next stage of their journey. The group of travellers found a quiet spot outside of the cave to sit and relax. They had each brought food for themselves. The next part of the journey would be to enter the Whispering Caves, which would be tricky, especially for those with insecurities. Jo had his concerns and thought it best to remind everyone about the cave.

"Legend has it that many travellers have gone mad from being in the Whispering Caves, as they believed what the caves were whispering to them," Jo explained, feeling anxious that his inner strength may fail him.

"This is going to be tough because we have no idea what the caves may whisper to us. It could even be connected to your insecurities, hidden deep within your subconscious," Jo aired his concern. The travellers ate in silence, mentally preparing their minds for the challenge ahead. This would be a true test of mind over matter.

***

Kyle knew their rest was to be short-lived, as there was no time to waste. They needed to arrive at Katia's stronghold by midnight, taking advantage of the Forbidden Underworlds' time for merriment, when the inhabitants would be in good spirits. It would be a strategic time to approach the camp. The travellers quickly packed their belongings and set off on their journey once again.

"I can't help but think we are being lulled into a false sense of security. I can't hear any whisperings in the cave," Bartholomew expressed as they entered.

Once inside, everything seemed ordinary until Kyle abruptly stopped in his tracks.

"Did one of you just speak to me?" Kyle asked, looking around the cave.

"I didn't hear anything," Carmel said, looking at the other travellers' faces for a response. They all shook their heads, indicating that they hadn't heard anything either.

"That will be the whisperers, Kyle. Just try to stay focused and dismiss what they say to you. They are here to deceive you; continue walking," Jo advised, patting Kyle's back. It was the best advice he could give, not just to Kyle, but to everyone else in the cave.

As they continued to walk, the whispers penetrated Kyle's mind and spoke softly to him.

"Kyle, Kyle, it's Ellie. Please come back; we need you here. I miss you, and I am scared. Please come back," the whisperings repeated, and Kyle could see Ellie in his mind. The whispers sucked him into believing the message, and he felt himself being pulled towards it.

The mood in the cave had changed, as the whisperings were now happening to all the travellers. None of them could hear each other's whisperings, only their own. Ravena had transformed back to her human form, perched on a rock as if she was deep in conversation with someone.

"Yes, I will fly and be free," Ravena whispered, influenced by the message.

Jo noticed the change in Ravena's behaviour and quickly approached.

"Ravena, snap out of it! It's the whisperers trying to deceive you. Don't listen to them!" he shouted, trying to break the hold of the whispers on her.

The other travellers, too, realised that they were under the influence of the whispers and began to shake off the deceptive messages, focusing on Jo's words and the task at hand - to keep moving and not succumb to the illusions created by the cave's whisperings.

***

Jo was now also in turmoil with his whisperings. He had not anticipated that they would feel so genuine in his mind. He could hear his daughter's voice telling him that she was still alive, and he needed to find her.

"Dad, I wish I could reach out and touch your face. I have missed you so much, but I am lost. On that dreadful day, I never died. As I floated down into the abyss of the water, something saved me. The thing that saved me has taken me to the place where the lost souls go. I tried to telepathically communicate with you, but you have never heard me. I can see you. I have seen my dear beloved Ellie turn into a beautiful intelligent girl who is following in my footsteps. You must find the psychic they call Shareena. She lives in our village. The reason you have never found my body is that I am still alive. Hurry, Dad, come find me."

Jo was now shouting in anguish. "No, no, it's not true, you're not real; go away!"

Jo shouted so loudly that it startled the group, abruptly pulling them out of their whisperings. They ran to Jo, who was holding his head in his hands, sobbing. Jasper, who had transformed back to his human form, was frantically rummaging around in his rucksack.

"I've found it! I brought some cotton wool with me. It's good for cleaning my hooves, but we can also use it to block out the whisperings," Jasper said excitedly, pulling the cotton wool from his rucksack. "If we place it in our ears, we won't be able to hear them clearly, and we won't be influenced by what they're saying."

The news of the cotton wool was a relief to them all. "If it helps to eliminate the personal torment we've been going through, it will be a blessing," Jo said, quickly placing the cotton wool in his ears.

Ravena and Carmel decided to walk on either side of Jo to provide him with some support. The whisperings were now reduced to a muffled sound within their minds, making the rest of the journey through the cave more bearable. However, Jo was left with what the whisperings had said to him.

***

The travellers reached the exit of the cave and stepped back into the night's crisp air. Up ahead, there was a town where singing and laughter could be heard. Queen Jamillia stood still, looking towards the town, knowing that she would soon be reunited with her husband, and they could put their plan into action.

"It sounds like the town is wide awake, and we'll get to meet up with Katia tonight. Remember, I am not their queen, and Katia holds that position. Is everyone ready for the last part of the journey? Let's go over our stories in our heads," Queen Jamillia said.

The group braced themselves for the cold weather, looking subdued and unprepared for the pretending they would need to do to partake in the festivities at the stronghold.

17

As Kyle approached the town, he could see that it was shrouded with an eerie, dense fog. It stretched out ahead of them like a wall, obscuring their view and creating an unsettling atmosphere. He knew that they would need to walk through this fog to reach Katia's stronghold.

"Does anyone know anything about this fog?" Kyle asked, pulling up the collar on his coat to shield himself from the biting cold. He wondered if Carmel's elixir was wearing off, leaving them vulnerable to the elements.

"I know a bit about the myths from the books I found in the town where Katia lives," Queen Jamillia shared, her voice slightly muffled by the dense fog. "The books refer to it as the place where the lost souls dwell."

Jo had a foreboding feeling as the group ventured further into the fog. The icy breaths and the sensation of being touched unnerved them all.

"Hey, Carmel, I thought that elixir stuff was supposed to keep us warm. I sure as hell feel cold right now," Jo said, shivering.

"I know, I'm cold too, and it's supposed to keep us warm. It's never failed before," Carmel replied, shivering along with the rest of the group.

They huddled together as they walked, trying to condense their body heat for warmth. Ravena circled above them, keeping an eye out for any unusual activity. Suddenly, she swooped down to re-join the group.

We are not alone," she spoke frantically. "There are around 30 people in this fog with us. They are just walking around aimlessly, murmuring to themselves."

A woman appeared in front of them, with dark circles under her eyes. Her hair was damp from the mist, and her skin was tinged blue from the cold. She walked up to Jo and looked into his eyes.

"She's here. Beth is here; if you look hard enough, you will find her."

Carmel interjected, rearing up between Jo and the woman. Her eyes flashed with anger.

"Stop! How dare you play with this man's mind! What makes you utter your cruel ramblings of a madwoman?"

The unknown woman did not flinch or move. "I only speak the truth. Beth is still alive. I have spoken with her. She knew you would be coming here. She said to show you this." The woman opened her hand and revealed a gold locket.

"That's my Beth's." Jo took the locket and opened it, revealing two pictures, one in each half. One was of Jo holding Beth as a baby, and the other was of Ellie.

"Where did you get it?" Jo clasped the locket in his hand, his heart beating rapidly. The woman spoke no more; she turned away and drifted back into the fog.

The group were stunned by what had happened. Jo told them that the whisperings in the cave had also told him that Beth was still alive.

"What if this is true? My Beth could be lost," Jo's voice trembled as he spoke. "The whisperings told me to find a lady called Shareena. I will find her when we get back."

Jo placed the locket in his pocket, feeling reassured that everything they were doing was right. Beth would have wanted him to pursue this mission for the good of the Underworld and Ellie.

The fog started to clear, revealing the sparkling lights of the town and the scent of roasting food filling their nostrils. They had a small hill to climb before reaching the entrance of the town.

***

Once they reached the top of the hill, Blue departed from the group as planned and wished them good luck. The town was protected by a large stone wall, and in the centre of the wall stood a wooden door with a wrought iron door knocker in the shape of a bear's head. Bartholomew reached up and pounded the knocker on the door, bracing himself to switch his personality to that of his brother.

A deep voice from the other side called out. "On behalf of the town of Lemuda, state who you are?" No niceties were offered with the request.

"It is Katia's faithful follower, Bernard; I have returned from Alaska. I have brought with me new volunteers for our cause."

The guard opened the door and embraced Bartholomew tightly in a bear hug. "Welcome back, Bernard. I didn't expect to see you so soon. I thought you were with the missus and the new baby." Bartholomew hugged the man back.

"You know what my woman is like. She said I was under her feet, and I was better off doing what I do best. In my case, that is making money." The guard gave the rest of the group suspicious glances and pulled Bartholomew to one side.

"What's with the group that you have brought with you? They better not be imposters. Where did you find them?" the guard demanded.

Bartholomew glanced back at the group, who now looked nervous. "Do you think I would have brought a group of imposters with me? No, that's not my style. You know how strict I am on security. Trust me, this lot wants to fight for our cause." Bartholomew's voice was confident as he defended the group. The guard looked at the motley crew and assessed them, while Kyle put on his most grimacing face.

"One of them is Queen Jamillia. As you know, her husband, King Jamari, is already here. She wants to join him too and she has managed to persuade some of her supporters to come with her. I told them I will take them to see Katia. They have important news to tell her." The guard looked the group up and down.

"Any friends of Bernard's are friends of mine. Welcome to our town, enjoy your stay." The group smiled back in acceptance of his welcoming gesture and hurried off into the town.

"Right, our next step is to go and find Gino Martini; nobody gets to speak with Katia without booking an appointment. A word of warning: don't get tricked into buying something from him. Gino is a master salesperson and will even try to sell you the ground on which you are walking. He's not a bad fellow," explained Bartholomew.

The group observed their surroundings; the town was bustling with activity, not what you would expect for midnight in a small town in the middle of the Forbidden Underworld.

**

"Hot potatoes, hot potatoes, come and get your spuds!" the market seller called out. Kyle stopped to observe the seller as she juggled hot potatoes in her bare hands.

"Come on, my lovely, try my hot potatoes; they're the best in town." Kyle waved off the woman's offer and declined her goods.

"Ouch, what was that?"

Kyle rubbed the back of his head, feeling pain and unsure of what had caused it. The potato seller had taken it upon herself to throw a hot potato at his head.

Bartholomew checked to see if Kyle was alright, observing him as he tried to wipe the potato from the back of his head.

"You need to watch out for those sellers, Kyle. It's highly competitive around here at this time of night. Best not to give them eye contact, they may take it as a go-ahead to sell to you and get angry when you refuse."

Bartholomew's advice had come a little too late for Kyle. He made a mental note to remember this. It didn't take long for him to put this advice into practice, as there were now vendors everywhere, selling everything from herbs to magic spells.

Entertainers of every type filled the streets - tightrope walkers, flamethrowers, and contortionists moving around in strange positions. There was even a wrestling match between a human and a bear, with a considerable crowd cheering, shouting, and waving money in the air to place bets on the winner. Bartholomew shook his head in disbelief at the spectacle before them.

"I can't believe they still fall for this scam," Bartholomew remarked. "The bear has never lost yet; he is the town's mascot. That's whose head is on the door knocker at the entrance of the town."

Up ahead, Carmel could see a big top with the words '*Formidable Circus - Enter at Your Own Peril*' written on it. At the side of the big top was a man on stilts.

"Roll up, roll up! Come and watch Mr Formidable's amazing circus!" The man on stilts wore a top hat and red and black tails and was trying his best to sell circus tickets to passers-by.

Bartholomew scanned the man up and down. "That's our man, Gino Martini; we must see him if we want an appointment with Katia tonight," Bartholomew said.

"He looks like a harmless chap, and it seems the town is having fun," Jo exclaimed.

"They do pride themselves on fun, but never underestimate them; most of them cannot be trusted," Carmel added solemnly.

As they approached Gino, Bartholomew spoke first. "Mr Martini, how are you feeling up there? I have brought new volunteers and need an urgent appointment with Katia. We bring important news."

Gino Martini stooped down without losing his balance. "Hello, Bernard, you're back! Can you not stay away from us? You say important news; it must be, because no one would dare ask to see Katia on her day off."

Gino turned to the group. "Welcome, newcomers."

He proceeded to take off his top hat in a welcoming gesture, bowing down to Carmel and offering her his hat. She was feeling amused at this point.

"Beautiful lady, charmed to meet you. Do you feel lucky? Please pick a card, any card. It could improve your life."

He pushed the top hat toward Carmel, and she started laughing. "I can't be conned by that old trick. It's a shame you didn't recognise me, or you would have used your scam on one of the others."

Gino bent down even further to observe her face. "Oh my, it's only little Carmel, gone and turned herself into a woman. I always knew you would return. Greetings, my fair lady." Gino bowed gracefully and placed his top hat back on his head.

"We'll catch up later. Bernard, if you go into the circus and nod at the ringmaster three times, he will know you are here to see Katia. Beware, though, one of you will have to perform a task in the show. If you complete it, your request to meet Katia will be granted. I bid you all an entertaining evening."

Kyle was not familiar with the Forbidden Underworld's antics and was puzzled over the failed card trick.

"Carmel, what was Gino going to do with the cards he offered you?"

Carmel tried to stifle a smile. She had been a good friend of Gino's when she was young and knew he was only trying to make a living.

"If it had been you, because you don't understand the ways here, he would have been about to con you into a binding agreement to buy something from him.

175

What that something was, would have depended on which card you had picked off him," Carmel explained.

"I'm glad Gino didn't target me. I don't fancy being bound to an agreement for something I don't want," Kyle sighed, wiping his brow with relief.

They joined the crowd and waited to enter the big top. It was a splendid tent with large blue and white stripes. There was all manner of creatures waiting, including demons. The demon families seldom showed up in the town, other than local councillors attending events to maintain good community relations. Carmel was relieved to see some prominent demon families attending.

The group entered the big top. Once inside, Bartholomew made eye contact with the ringmaster and nodded three times. The ringmaster responded with three nods.

Everyone sat down and the ringmaster entered the big top and bellowed, "Please be standing and welcome our hostess for the night, your almighty leader, Katia."

The crowd stood and cheered frantically as Katia entered. She looked impressive, dressed in a long purple fitted dress, with a velvet hooded cape.

As Katia looked into the crowd, her violet eyes gave out a hypnotising glare. Carmel couldn't help but think, despite her fear, that Katia looked beautiful, almost like an ethereal spirit.

"Welcome, my followers. Please be seated and enjoy the show. I will be available to speak to a selected few after the performances. You will be collected by one of my trusted assistants, so remain seated if you have requested to speak with me. Let the show begin."

There was a large boom as the spectacular pyrotechnics erupted inside the big top. Katia made her way to her throne-styled seat.

The lights dimmed in the big top, and the atmosphere felt electric as the crowd waited in anticipation for the show to start. Fang began to feel on edge, and his hackles went up, sensing something amiss.

Fake smoke filled the circular arena of the big top. The sound of three wolves howling in unison echoed through the air. As the smoke cleared, they had transformed into three women, dressed in silver evening dresses with their dark hair cascading down to their waists. The crowd gasped in awe as the three she-wolves began to sing in perfect angelic harmony.

One of the she-wolves left and approached Fang, staring into his eyes. Fang, who was already in human form, got up from his seat and walked with the she-wolf to the stage.

She whispered in his ear, "Sing for me and Katia will welcome you."

Reluctantly, Fang opened his mouth, and an enchanting tenor voice echoed through the acoustics of the tent. Katia watched him intently as the crowd cheered with excitement. Fang returned to his seat, feeling uncomfortable with the attention.

Gino had pre-warned them that there would be a task to complete if they wanted a private meeting with Katia. Fang glanced in Katia's direction, and she nodded to him, acknowledging her seal of approval.

18

The crowd sat and chatted as the stage was set up for the next act. Four metal hoops were placed in the centre of the arena. The ringmaster lit the hoops, there was a drum roll, and King Jamari strolled out. He bowed his head to the people and began jumping through the burning hoops. Queen Jamillia wanted to walk out.

"This is so against everything we stand for, everything we believe in. Why is Jamari doing this?" Queen Jamillia muttered to Ravena in dismay, as the crowd cheered loudly when the ringmaster announced the next act.

"Give a loud round of applause and welcome the Black Pioneers and the amazing bareback acrobats!"

Twelve black horses bounded in with six male and six female acrobats balancing on their backs. Their routine had been practised to the highest standard with impeccable timing.

The acrobats performed handstands on the horses' backs and jumped from one horse to another. They finished their show by synchronising perfect backflips off the horses' backs. The grand finale was when the horses stood on their hind legs and reared up in perfect time to the music, as if they were dancing.

***

No sooner had the crowd stopped applauding than the dancers arrived in the circle. They were dressed in white performer outfits, and every time the lighting changed, so did the colour of their costumes.

"Got to admit, they know how to put on an impressive show," Kyle whispered to Jasper.

Seeing the Black Pioneers made Jasper feel uneasy, given his past with them. It had been a long time since he ran with them, but he knew he would have to run with them once again.

The ringmaster took the stage to thank the acts in the show. For the finale, they all bowed as pyrotechnics filled the tent. The crowd gasped as the tent's ceiling opened, revealing the black sky filled with hundreds of fireworks, lighting it up. As the show ended, the group waited for Katia's assistant to approach them. They didn't have to wait long before one of the glamorous showgirls walked over to them.

"Please follow me. Katia will see you," the dancer said, leading the travellers to a smaller tent.

Jasper was beginning to feel anxious about being in the presence of his past abuser. The tent resembled a Bedouin tent and was luxuriously decorated with purple satin, and the scent of burning incense filled the air. Purple cushions were scattered randomly throughout the tent, and Katia sat in a trance on one of them.

"Please, come in and make yourselves comfortable. We have much to discuss," said Katia, opening her violet eyes and gazing at her visitors as they took their seats.

"Ah, yes, some of you I am already acquainted with, but what I cannot understand is why some of the Underworld's most trusted followers are now in my presence." Jasper realised that Katia wouldn't recognise him in his human form.

"Bernard, I am glad to have your trusted and loyal service back. The six men I have had to employ in your place are no match for the level of security you provide," Katia stated. "How is the baby? Gino has already explained that your wife would rather have you working. If you would like, I can send one of my assistants to aid her in Alaska." Katia tapped the table with her talon-like nails, waiting for a response.

"No assistance is needed, Katia. My wife has her family with her, and I fear it would make my mother-in-law feel incompetent if I sent someone else. That's partly the reason why I returned. They are all fussing around her like mother hens, but thank you for the offer."

"Very well, Bernard. I respect your wishes." Katia turned away from Bartholomew.

"Queen Jamillia, I have the courtesy and honour to welcome you. Please remember that we are not here to compete. Your status and title will be upheld, and I will make sure every member of my town does the same. As you know, your husband is already here with us." The Queen cringed inside, trying to hide her disdain for Katia.

"Queen Jamillia, what is it that persuaded you to join our cause?" Katia asked, her tone measured and composed.

Despite her anger, Queen Jamillia composed herself. "I am here to seek allies in our mission to protect and educate humans about the animal kingdom. We need to find a way to coexist and respect the balance of nature." Katia listened intently, her eyes narrowing slightly.

"I know my husband wants to do what he feels is right to avenge his family and kin. We are dwindling in numbers, and he feels the great need to fight to survive, so after much thought, I cannot deny him my support," Queen Jamillia said, her voice resolute. Jo nodded in agreement with the Queen's statement.

"Hear, hear! We are here to fight to defend the animal kingdom, and we will do what it takes to preserve it," he said passionately.

Katia stood up and applauded Jo, showing her appreciation for his words.

"What fine words you speak, a man after my own heart, and fight you will. I see you have brought your weapon of choice. May I enquire which organisation you have been a member of in the Underworld?" Katia asked, her curiosity piqued.

Jo had not thought about how to answer this question, and he didn't believe it would be wise to make up an organisation, considering Katia's many business contacts. However, he was relieved that she thought he was from the Underworld.

"None. I am independent, and my only wish is to join the Forbidden Underworld's organisation and the band of archers. In the Underworld, I am a master archer, but there is not much use for it nowadays, mostly only for recreational purposes. I heard through the grapevine that you needed strong fighters, the best, and here I am," Jo said as he stood up in front of Katia and bowed to her.

"Charmed, and what name do you go by?"

"The Grand Archer," Jo responded.

Katia seemed delighted by his answer. "The Grand Archer is how you shall be known by all who reside here," she declared.

Fang decided to go next, knowing it would be difficult to act loyal. He prowled over to Katia, staying in his wolf form, as he knew she was fond of wolves. She surrounded herself with them and even used them for hunting and killing. Fang stopped by her side and looked up at her.

"Fang, you have been sadly missed here by your pack," Katia said, addressing him. "Your she-wolf has pined for you many nights, howling in the hope you would return. Please go gently with her. You have been away a long time, and she will be hostile to you. I feel that before you do battle with the humans and the Underworld, you have your own battle to endure with your she-wolf." Fang bowed his head, knowing that it would be a brutal fight.

"I only hope, Fang, that it will not be too savage. I would hate to lose either of you," Katia said softly. "I knew you would return; a lone wolf does not make a happy wolf." She ran her fingers through his fur and bent down to his ears.

"If you leave or betray us again, your pack will turn on you; that is something you need to consider deeply," Katia warned with a firm tone. Fang did not like the threat, but he chose to show his loyalty by resting his head at her feet.

"Carmel, your presence here puzzles me deeply. You have not harmed anyone or shown any demonic behaviour for a long time. Please tell me why you are here?"

Lying came easily to Carmel. It was in her blood and nature to tap into her demonic traits whenever she wanted. However, she hadn't used those traits for a while, as she preferred to keep her anger in check.

"Yes, Katia, I was incredibly happy with my husband. You know he is a good man. Frannie has helped me for many years to control my temper, but now he has left me. He caught me using my powers on another human that had angered me and he will not accept or tolerate what I have done. I have found myself wanting to return more and more to my old ways," Carmel explained, her voice tinged with sadness as she spun her tale of woe.

Carmel hated the lies she was telling, and a pang of longing for her dear Frannie pierced her heart. She knew she had to tread carefully and maintain her façade, but the pain of deception weighed heavily on her.

"I had a hunger to return here, it has been burning away inside of me, and now I have returned. I hope you will welcome me back. You do not have many of my kind in the town, and I can be beneficial in helping you reach out to the larger demon community." Carmel spoke with confidence, carefully choosing her words to present herself as a valuable asset to Katia's cause.

Despite her inner turmoil, Carmel maintained a composed demeanour, determined to play her part convincingly. She waited for Katia's response with bated breath, hoping her words had found their mark. Katia paused, studying Carmel intently before speaking.

"Yes, Carmel, my relations with the demon community are somewhat fractious. You, however, are different; you were raised here in this town until your mother decided to take you into the Underworld. You have first-hand knowledge of our way of life, and you could mediate our cause to the demon world. You also have good knowledge of the Under and Upperworld and some of their immoral ways. Therefore, I accept you."

As each member was accepted, the travellers began to feel more relaxed.

Ravena remained in her human form as she awaited her turn to speak to Katia.

"My reasons are straightforward, Katia. The Forbidden Underworld was my home, but as a shapeshifter, it was harder for me to fit in with the other ravens. Many of them choose not to shapeshift, seeing it as a crime within the raven community. If I join your community, it won't be far for me to fly to join with my kind. I can also travel to the Underworld and Upperworld with great efficiency and speed. No one will suspect me of being anything other than a raven. My ability to spy for you and report back will be a great asset. So, if you accept, I would like to be your eyes and ears."

Ravena transformed into her bird form, flew, and landed on Katia's shoulder, demonstrating her loyalty. Katia nodded in approval.

Jasper had also stayed in human form.

"What about you?" Katia asked, admiring Jasper's good looks.

His face was unshaven, giving him a rugged look, coupled with his long black hair and white streak, it made him attractive to the eye. It was hard for Jasper to proceed. He still bore the scars from Katia's cold, callous hands.

"I was one of your Black Pioneers, and one day I refused to perform in your show. Do you remember?" Jasper said, his voice tinged with bitterness.

Katia spun her head around to look at Jasper again, memories flooding back of using her whip to punish him when he was in horse form.

"My word, Jasper. Maybe if you had stayed in human form, we could have had a better working relationship," Katia remarked casually. Her words sickened him to the core, and the rest of the group looked on edge. Jasper was in danger of blowing their cover before they had even begun their mission.

"So, Jasper, why have you returned?" Katia asked.

"I have returned because humans treated me no better than you did," replied Jasper, his voice filled with contempt. "They rode me, kept me in stables, and controlled every aspect of my life. I needed to choose a side with a battle coming. I stand a better chance of achieving freedom with you and your followers." Jasper's words were calculated, as he knew that by aligning with Katia and her cause, he could potentially save some of the Black Pioneers from enslavement.

Katia rarely took pity on anything or anyone; she smiled, humouring him.

"Poor, poor Jasper. Do you want to be free?" Katia's words were laced with a sarcastic tone. "Well, there is no freedom in this world, so you must just put up with it and work hard. The Black Pioneers work extremely hard for me. Why should you be any different?"

Kyle interrupted, sensing that Jasper was on the verge of walking out and forgetting the bigger picture of why they were there.

"I apologise for interrupting, but we have some important information that you may find greatly beneficial," Kyle interjected. "You may be wondering why I am here. You know who I am and that I was brought up by the Underworld, but that is the only loyalty I have to them. I don't owe them anything." Katia listened intently to Kyle's words.

"We have a new elemental at the Underworld. One more powerful than I am. They are now focusing all their attention and energy on training her," Kyle continued. Katia quickly raised her hand to stop him from speaking.

"You're saying she's here? The final elemental, the fire element? The Underworld now has all four elementals, making them stronger than anything in the world. So, why would you choose to walk away from that power?" Kyle stood up and paced around the room.

"Because I'm jealous of her," Kyle admitted, his voice low. "Before she came, I was important, but now they only focus on her. It's even worse since her transformation day. Everyone's so excited about her powers, calling her the key elemental. I don't want to combine my powers with hers or with the other elementals. I want to be unique on my own."

Katia studied Kyle intently, and his words resonated with her. She saw in him a reflection of her past desires for power. She had always been driven by the ambition to possess all the elementals and harness their power for her gain. Now that she had one of them in her presence, it would have to suffice for the time being. Having one elemental was better than having none, and she was determined to make the most of it.

"Well, it looks like I have some new members to welcome," Katia said with a smile. "I'm sure you're all tired and could use some rest. It's extremely late, and we have a lot of planning to do over the next few days." Katia motioned for her assistant. "Take our new friends to the Old Inn."

The inn lived up to its name - it was old, and even the innkeeper was elderly. He came out to greet them, with his jolly red cheeks and greying hair, which he styled with long sideburns. He shuffled up the stairs, signalling for his guests to follow him.

"We're a bit full tonight with the circus in town," he explained. "I'm afraid some of you will have to share rooms." Queen Jamillia, Carmel, and Ravena were given one room, while Jo and Kyle were assigned to another. Fang and Jasper had the room next to them.

Bartholomew had left them outside the inn and made his way to Bernard's home in the village. He had arranged to meet them all in the morning. Once they had settled into their comfortable rooms, there was little time for conversation as the weary travellers were exhausted. Yet, despite their exhaustion, there was a palpable sense of contentment that their plan to infiltrate Katia's stronghold had succeeded.

19

Back in the Underworld, a lone figure hastily packed a bag, with too many thoughts running through their head.

"*How dare they tell me that I cannot go with them. No one tells me what to do*," Amber thought to herself.

The ground rumbled underneath her feet; her temper had gotten the better of her, and she needed to gain control quickly to avoid triggering an earthquake. All she wanted to do was help the Underworld. Amber knew the exact route the group had taken.

If the Grand Council was not going to permit her to join them, she would find the group herself. By the time anyone noticed she was missing, it would be too late. The Underworld would not risk sending another group to look for her.

Undeterred, Amber was determined to follow her friends' path. She believed that no one could control her, and her powers were strong enough to scare off any attacker. She soon encountered her first obstacle: the heavy door to the Forbidden Underworld. Fortunately, Amber had found an extra set of keys in the Grand Council's office, but she struggled to push open the door. She decided to use her powers. Amber placed her hand on the door, closed her eyes, and focused. The ground began to loosen, causing the door to shake and move just enough for her to squeeze through.

Amber's next obstacle was the three entrances, she began to panic.

"Which one should I choose?" Amber was determined not to be defeated and needed to think on her feet. She wondered, "*What would Blue do in this situation?*". Looking around, she noticed the imprints of footsteps at the entrance of the middle cave.

"That's the one I need", she decided. Taking a deep breath, she walked towards the middle cave and pulled up the hood of her cloak, as if it was some form of protection. It was easier for Amber to hide in the shadows and quickly make her way through the caves than it had been for the group.

Amber managed to navigate the cave skilfully, unnoticed by any demon child or dragon. She arrived at the cave where the Rock Men lived and the narrow tunnel where her companions had fought earlier. However, the Rock Men were on high alert and wary of any intruders. They had already lost 20 men during the fight with Bartholomew and Jasper, and they were determined not to lose any more. They spotted Amber before she even knew they were there.

The Rock Men had overheard the earlier group's conversation and knew that they were headed to Katia's stronghold. They also knew that this young traveller, Amber, was going to join them. To the Rock

Men, this was an opportunity to exact revenge on the group for destroying their men.

They waited silently, nodding to each other and grabbed her before she could run. Despite her physical strength, Amber was no match for the Rock Men. She could have used her powers to cause an earthquake, but she knew it would be too dangerous and put her own life at risk if the cave collapsed. Besides, nobody knew where she was, and she could end up trapped for a long time.

The Rock Men mocked Amber, "Where do you think you're going, young lady? To find your friends? Well, we don't think so. You're coming with us."

Amber felt a pang of fear as she asked, "Where are you taking me? Get off me, you bullies!" The Rock Men did not budge, they stood their ground firmly.

"We're taking you to Katia, and we'll let her know about your plans. You're in trouble now, young lady," one of the Rock Men said in a tone that irritated Amber.

"Shut up, you idiots," Amber snapped back. "You can't even move out of your rock cave, and everyone knows that. So how do you propose to get me out of here?"

Despite her resistance, the Rock Men pushed her up the narrow tunnel towards their destination.

"We can force ourselves out in an emergency, and we deem this as something that puts the Forbidden Underworld at risk. So, I am declaring this an emergency," said one of the two Rock Men.

Amber desperately looked for a way to escape the clutches of the Rock Men. She tried to stay calm, knowing that losing her temper would only make the situation worse. She didn't know what she feared the most: the wrath of Katia, the Rock Men, or the disappointment of the Underworld.

Out in the open, Amber was glad for the fresh air. She took in a deep breath to stop herself from having a panic attack. They approached the Valley of Lost Souls. There would be no danger of the souls harassing Amber while she was with the Rock Men, since they did not have the same level of consciousness as humans. They could have approached Amber, but instead, they hid in the shadowy fog and watched them walk by.

They arrived at the town's door and knocked.

"Who seeks entry to our town?" a voice from inside enquired. The Rock Men appeared, proud of their bounty.

"We, the Rock Men. We have captured an imposter who we believe has information on others that have already infiltrated your town. Please hear us out." The heavy door opened and the guard frowned at Amber.

"I will have some guards come and take you to Katia immediately," he said, and sounded an alarm that echoed throughout the town, deafening Amber.

In the distance, four black horses pulled an enclosed carriage that raced towards them, their hooves thundering into the ground. As the carriage and horses came to an abrupt stop, the guard spoke to the Rock Men.

"Get in the carriage and take your prisoner. The horses will take you to Katia's house." The chassis of the carriage almost touched the ground with the weight of the Rock Men, but the horses had enough power to easily pull them.

The horses and carriage came to a stop outside a large, foreboding house with a dark exterior fashioned with black shutters. Amber felt a wave of fear as she realised she would have to enter it. The absence of sunlight made the house look even more oppressive. The darkness had truly set in.

A guard opened the door and escorted them to a room.

"Please wait here until Katia is ready to see you." The Rock Men looked incredibly pleased with themselves over their capture as they waited to gain favour with Katia.

"I hope she will let us stay here in the town. I don't want to go back to the caves." The other Rock Man shrugged his massive stone shoulders.

"I don't know, she might."

Amber scanned the room, uninterested in the conversation. The room was a study, with shelves of books lining the walls. Shouting could be heard coming from the corridor just outside the room.

"Where is the imposter? How dare she think she can make her way towards my town. Who caught her?"

The door slammed open, hitting the wall, and cracking it. Katia stormed into the room and looked like a crazed woman. Amber recoiled and wished the ground would swallow her up. She started to focus on creating a minor earthquake, just enough to cause a commotion so she could find the rest of the group and escape. Katia continued to bellow.

"STOP! You foolish girl, did you think I would let you use your powers here without my permission? You are in my world now, little girl, and your powers will remain blocked until I decide to let you use them."

Amber knew she had caused a disastrous situation, and there was no way out of it. The most worrying part for Amber was that Katia would use her like a puppet.

"Good work, Rock Men. You will be made honorary key holders to my town. You may come and go as you wish or even choose to live here with your families. You have saved my town from a destructive plan of sabotage. Was the child travelling alone?" One of the Rock Men stood up and bowed to address Katia.

"Yes, ma'am, she was travelling alone. That's how we managed to capture her, but we're afraid that the group of people who came before the girl, managed to evade our attack. We lost several good men in the onslaught. They must pay the price."

Katia was reeling with anger. Amber feared for her life and tried to make a run for it. Katia caught hold of her and grabbed her by the throat, causing Amber to gasp for air. After a moment, Katia slowly released her grip.

"It is lucky for you that I need you alive. Your powers will aid me strongly in my battle." Katia placed one of her talon-like fingernails on Amber's cheek and ran it along the surface, drawing blood. Amber winced in pain from the burning sensation.

"Let this be a lesson to you. Never think you are clever enough to take me on. With just one finger, I could disfigure that pretty face of yours." Katia pushed Amber to the floor.

"Guards, come take the girl to the lair of the Div and the Deem; throw her in the pit. Instruct them to watch over her at all times, until I decide my next plan of action. Also, gather eight more of my guards to collect the rest of the imposters and bring them here to me."

Two guards dragged a sobbing Amber from the room and marched her out into the chilly air toward the pit. The Div and Deem snarled at Amber, circling her with saliva dripping from their fangs.

"Get away from me!" Amber cried and kicked out at the hideous creatures. The guards laughed at her feeble attempt to defend herself.

"I wouldn't do that if you value your legs. I've seen them take a man's leg off with one clean bite." The guard told the creatures to back off from Amber.

"Katia wants this one alive, so no lunch for you today." Amber watched as the creatures backed off from her, still snarling.

The guard ushered Amber over to a large pit in the ground.

"That's where you will be staying until further instruction from Katia," he said. Amber thought he would push her in, but she was relieved to see him retrieve a rope ladder and motion for her to climb down it.

"Down you go. We can't have you hurting yourself, we need you to be strong. I'm sure you'll have company soon when Katia's finished with the rest of the imposters." She descended down the ladder slowly, grateful for her warm cloak as the bottom of the pit was icy cold.

Amber had not been lucky enough to receive Carmel's elixir. All she could do now was stay calm and wait for the others to join her, and then try to explain her foolish actions. She looked up at the top of the pit; the Div and the Deem had circled the entrance in case she attempted to escape, but the guard had removed the rope ladder, so her chances of escape were slim.

***

The group woke up to the sound of loud knocking on the door of the Old Inn. They rushed out into the corridor, with Kyle being the last one to exit the room.

"Who do you think they're after? It sounds urgent," he asked.

The innkeeper opened the door, and eight guards dressed in black with their hair tied back in ponytails barged into the inn. Jasper, from the top of the stairs, watched them enter the foyer.

"It must be trouble, it's the Black Pioneers. Katia only sends out her elite guards when there is a threat to the town."

The innkeeper was trembling. "I have paid all my taxes up to date. What do you want with me?"

The Black Pioneers looked around the foyer. "Where are the imposters that came to stay here?"

The innkeeper pointed to the upstairs; he was too scared to talk. Ravena quickly transformed into her raven form, and Carmel opened the inn window for her to fly out.

"Go quickly, fly back to the Underworld, and tell them about our danger."

Ravena flew as fast as she could, and by the time the Black Pioneers reached upstairs, she was nowhere to be seen in the dark sky.

Jo used his compact mirror-tracking device to contact Ellie.

"Ellie, if you can hear me, get ready. We're under attack, and the Underworld needs to prepare. They know we're imposters. I can't use this device right now; if they figure out what it is, they'll use it to track you. I love you." Jo threw the mirror on the ground and shattered it, rendering it unusable.

"They're up here," shouted one of the Black Pioneers as they ran upstairs to capture the group.

There was no time for them to escape, as the drop from the inn window was too high for some members to make. Staying together in numbers gave them the best chance of survival. The group had no choice but to surrender, as they were not prepared for battle.

Jasper chose not to transform into a horse, as he would have been vastly outnumbered by the eight Black Pioneers. They may have even killed him for deserting. Kyle and Carmel attempted to use their powers but found them to be ineffective. As soon as Katia became aware of the imposters in her town, she used her telepathic mind control to block all their powers, as she had with Amber. Fang stayed in his human form this time; he felt stronger facing Katia as a man.

None of the group knew how they had been found out. They remained silent as the Black Pioneers escorted them out of the Old Inn. The innkeeper scowled at them.

"Where are the other two? There are supposed to be eight of you," asked one of the Black Pioneers. The group decided to maintain their silence.

"Have it your way. You'll soon be talking when Katia gets hold of you," threatened one of the Black Pioneers.

The group looked at each other, stunned as to what was happening. They were still unaware that Amber had followed them. They arrived at Katia's house and were pushed into the same room where Amber had been earlier.

"I should have known it was too good to be true. Guards, go fetch Bernard. I believe he is at his dwelling. I would like to know if he is part of this pathetic masquerade," said Katia.

Kyle was relieved that she was still unaware that Bernard was Bartholomew. At least one of them could stay in the town and spy on Katia.

"You are missing a member. Where are they?" Katia asked, but the group remained silent and shrugged their shoulders.

***

"First, I want to question Bernard. He brought all of you here." A strained-looking Bartholomew entered the room. He quickly assessed the situation from the group's body language and knew it didn't look good.

"How can I help you, Katia? I was having breakfast when your guards barged in on me," Bartholomew replied, trying to play it safe and act as normal as possible.

"Bernard, did you know what was going on? Or are you in on this with this group of imposters?" Katia asked, staring at him.

"No, I knew nothing about them being imposters. I had no idea."

Bartholomew was worried about his situation. He knew he was physically strong but not strong enough to take on the whole of the town. This could only end up with people getting hurt, and he now feared for the safety of his companions, who had not said a word since he had entered the room.

"I am not convinced, Bernard. So, let me make it clear how serious this situation is. I have taken it upon myself to bring your wife and child from Alaska. A pack of wolves is preparing to go and collect them."

Bartholomew looked at the rest of the group, wishing they could help him. He knew his brother would find out about his deception and would be enraged to know that he had tried to ruin his reputation with Katia. Bartholomew had put Bernard's wife and child at risk. He realised that the only solution would be to confess his identity.

He had noticed that Ravena was not with the group and guessed that she had already flown for help, so there was at least a chance that they would be rescued.

"Okay, I will come clean. I am not Bernard. I am his twin, Bartholomew. I can assure you that my brother has nothing to do with our plans to enter your town as imposters. Take me prisoner but leave my brother alone." Katia laughed mockingly.

"Bartholomew, when will you learn? I don't think you are in any position to negotiate any terms with me. I will have the wolves I have sent bring your brother and ask him how he thinks I should deal with you. I have been betrayed by all of you, and you leave me with no choice but to send you to the pit. You'll find you will be in good company with another traitor."

***

Carmel looked terrified. Most people who ended up at the pit were usually banished to the Valley of Lost Souls, to remain lost forever in the fog. This had certainly not been what she had planned for her life. She missed Frannie, so much.

The guards tied the prisoners' hands together behind their backs as a precaution in case they tried to fight back. They had called on the Rock Men to assist them in escorting the prisoners to the pit. The Rock Men were eager to gloat and humiliate the prisoners.

"We meet again. You thought you had defeated us, but we defeated you. We caught your little friend and beat you in the end." Carmel was worried by their chanting and thought they must have caught Ravena.

Kyle was the first to break the silence. "Shut up. What did you do? Follow us here so you could tell tales to Katia. You have ruined the chances of a good future for many people and animals. We came here to help. You are the traitors. Just you wait, Rock Men. You will be on the wrong side of history. Don't think that because you have caught Ravena, the Underworld will not be alerted to our captivity."

The Rock Men roared with laughter. "We caught ourselves a real gem," they jeered. Bartholomew wanted to hit out at them, but there were too many guards, and he valued his own life and the lives of his companions.

As they approached the pit, they could see the Div and the Deem circling and snarling down at the prisoner.

"Clear the way, we have the rest of the imposters," the guards ordered, pushing past the Div and the Deem.

"Help!" a familiar voice echoed out of the pit. "It's me, Amber." The group was shocked and dismayed to hear that Amber was also in the pit.

"Amber, what are you doing here?" Carmel was confused.

The guards pushed the prisoners forward. "Save your talking for when you're down in the pit with your traitor friend. We have a meeting and a battle to plan. Katia will put you all to effective use, so you'll get your imposter wish and will now be made to fight for us." The group was forced to climb down the rope ladder where Amber was waiting for them.

They sat huddled together on the damp pit floor and turned their focus towards Amber. Kyle had been close to Amber for a long time as a friend. He sat next to her, and even though he was angry inside, he did not think the best approach was to go in with all guns blazing. A softer approach was needed. Amber hung her head in shame and trembled in fear. Tears poured down her dusty face, leaving it streaked.

"Amber, what were you thinking? The Grand Council had very good reasons to tell you that you couldn't come on the mission. It was seen as too dangerous to risk another elemental, and this proves it. Do you know that Katia has used her telepathic abilities to block us from using our powers? So, we are useless."

Fang turned himself into a wolf and sat next to Amber. "Keep close to me, Amber, my fur will keep you warm." The rest of the group still had the effects of the elixir keeping them warm.

Jo tried to ease the situation and offer some hope.

"All we can do now is wait. I have sent word to Ellie, and Ravena has flown off to inform the Underworld of our fate. So, we must have hope they will make plans to rescue us all." The group fell silent as the darkness above offered them no comfort.

20

Ellie ran so fast that her feet didn't touch the ground. She had been sitting at home when she received Grandpa Jo's message through the compact mirror, and she hadn't been able to contact him since.

Ellie made her way down the hatch to the Underworld and didn't stop to speak to anyone as she headed towards the grand hall, which was bustling with activity. The expressions on their faces told her that they had already heard what had happened.

Ravena stood at the front of the hall, frantically talking to Bob Bomtane. On her way back, she noticed that the door separating the Underworld from the Forbidden Underworld was already open. Ravena alerted the Grand Council that someone had either entered or left the Underworld, and fear and panic set in. Bob sent a small team to shut the door and investigate further.

The hall was packed to full capacity. Bill made his way over to his daughter, giving her a big hug.

"I'm so scared, Dad. I hope Grandpa is safe."

"Order, order!" Bob Bomtane banged his gavel on his sound block repeatedly. The room fell silent, and everyone waited for his words.

"Most of you have probably already heard the news, but for those who haven't, our volunteers have been captured, and their whereabouts are currently undisclosed." Cries of concern were heard throughout the hall from loved ones and friends. Ellie held back her tears.

"Ravena has bravely offered to fly back to find out what is happening. We also have a severe security issue that is currently being handled by one of our tracker teams led by Blue. The door to the Underworld was left open, and Blue assured me he had shut it upon his return. We are not sure at this moment if someone has entered or left. So, until we have more information, keep your eyes and ears open, and please report any suspicious activity."

As Bob spoke, there was movement in the hall, and Blue and his team made their way up to where he was standing.

"Has anyone seen Amber, or have any idea where she is?" Blue enquired.

Nobody in the hall could confirm Amber's whereabouts. According to a member of the crowd, the last sighting of Amber was the day before.

"I saw her leaving one of the classrooms yesterday. She was wearing the same hooded cloak she had on at the emergency meeting. She didn't speak to me or seem to notice me but hurried past as if she was in a rush to get somewhere."

"We have a more serious problem than any of us could have imagined. We believe that Amber entered the Forbidden Underworld of her own accord. She may have been captured along with the other volunteers. If this is true, Katia will have access to the powers of two elementals and can use them as she wishes. If she manipulates these powers, it will not bode well for the world. I fear that a storm is brewing, and it will bring disastrous times."

A member of the crowd interrupted Blue with his heckling. "What can we do? We need to go and retrieve our people immediately and not delay their return any further." Tensions were rising in the hall, and Ellie was upset with herself for not having noticed that Amber was missing.

Bob tried to keep the peace. "Please remember that we still have two elementals here who can assist us, including Ellie, who is not only an elemental but also a key to our salvation. We will be calling on many of you to help us plan and prepare our strategy over the next few days, so I ask that you remain calm." The weight of obligation for Ellie to be the Underworld's salvation made her feel uncomfortable.

"However, this does not make her superior to anyone else. Her unique gifts can be utilised for the greater good, if they are placed in the right hands. Please make your way home, get some rest, and await our call. If we need your assistance, we will inform you. Thank you, and goodnight." Bob frowned; he was clearly concerned about the situation.

The hall cleared, leaving behind a small group consisting of Frannie, Bill, Ellie, Blue, and Lady Marabelle, who stayed to assist in devising a rescue plan. Blue, an expert in strategy, contributed some ideas.

"I believe we all agree that we need to start working on a strategic plan immediately. There is another way to enter the Forbidden Underworld, and that is by travelling through the catacombs in the Boggopods. It will be quicker and safer. There is a secret passage we can use, but it is heavily guarded, so we will need to fight to get to the town. They will be vigilant about an impending attack, so the chances of sneaking in and out are not likely. We need to take our best fighters and weapons." Ellie had faith in Blue's planning skills, but she lacked confidence in her ability to fight, despite having undergone training.

***

Katia sat quietly in her darkened room, knowing that her town was well-guarded and that she had two of the elementals on her side. Despite this, she knew the Underworld would come with a strong fighting force. She could do nothing but wait for their attack.

In the meantime, a team of wolves was on their way to Alaska to fetch Bernard and expose his brother's deceit to him. Katia was confident Bernard would return to assist her, as he had always been loyal to her town. She had instructed the wolves to offer him a substantial salary increase to come back as the head of her security. Additionally, Katia summoned Carmel. It was time to start utilising her captives. Carmel arrived, looking dishevelled and exhausted.

"Carmel, you must come with me to the neighbouring town, to speak with the head of the demons. We need all the help we can get. Tell them that I have welcomed you here graciously and that the Underworld plans to attack our town. We need their help to defend ourselves."

Carmel was too scared to argue, and she knew her powers had been limited, so resisting was futile. She hadn't been to the demon village since she was a little girl, and the thought of going back was an unbearable task, one she didn't want to undertake.

***

Back in the Underworld, people had come from all over the planet via the toboggans. Ellie observed a group of monks that had arrived and who were expressing concern for the safety of the animal kingdom. These monks had maintained solid communication and liaisons with the Grand Council for years.

It was a crucial aspect of their belief system that animals and all life should be highly revered. The monks were also renowned worldwide as experts in martial arts. A group of 30 monks had been sent to protect and aid the Underworld during their battle with the Forbidden Underworld. As Ellie watched curiously, the master monk addressed Bob. "We have come from the temple hidden in the mountains. We are not warriors in war, but we are committed to defending and protecting what we believe is worth saving. Our rigorous training has given us bodies of steel, and we will make a good defence team for you.

Our primary goal is to prevent any loss of life in battle. However, if death befalls us, we firmly believe that it is just a new beginning in a new form."

The monks, dressed in orange robes and with clean-shaven heads, each carried a staff and monk spade. Bob Bomtane expressed his gratitude for the monks' help.

"Thank you. Your support is most welcome, and we will set up sleeping arrangements in the classrooms for you. You are also welcome to use the recreation room for training. I do have a question for you: are your bodies really as strong as steel?"

"Yes, it is true. Years of dedicated training and discipline have given us many strengths. You must come and watch us train; we will give you some lessons," said the master monk. Bob watched as one of the monks in the distance performed a no-handed cartwheel.

He laughed wholeheartedly. "I think I will leave the training to you. I am not agile enough to fly through the air," Bob said as he smiled at the monk.

The monk bowed with his hands together and re-joined his group. Ellie had to admit that she, too, would be missing training with the monks since it was far too strenuous for her capabilities.

***

Katia was about to set off to the demon town with Carmel when she heard a commotion outside her home.

"He's coming back! Asamara returns!"

The cheers from the town could be heard. Katia rushed to the door of her house, stepping out onto the dusty path. If the cheers were right, her father was back. She felt a sense of fear, even though he was her father. She always felt like nothing she did was good enough. This time, she was sure she was in for one of his angry outbursts. The sound of the horses' hooves was deafening as 12 Black Pioneers pulled the two stagecoaches.

On the side of each coach, in large gold letters, were the initials A.P. The first coach pulled up, and the six black horses stood tall, wearing black plumed dressage. The Black Pioneers had taken it upon themselves to find their Lord Asamara and inform him of the imminent danger to the town. Asamara had brought allies with him, who would help plan an attack on the Underworld.

The doors opened, and the passengers stepped out. Ahriman, Morag the Hag, and Dazi Haka. The second coach pulled up carrying Vidatu, Jahi, and Asamara. The town members cheered as if royalty had descended upon them, but Katia did not share their enthusiasm for her father's arrival and was unhappy with his presence.

The group walked towards Katia, and her father approached her with no love or compassion displayed.

"Meeting in the house, now," he said coldly as he walked past her. Vidatu, the Demon of Death, pushed past Katia, emitting a mist of green vapour from the corner of his mouth as he grimaced at her.

"Good evening, Katia. You look as beautiful as ever," said Ahriman, his hypnotising blue eyes fixed on her.

Jahi, who was standing beside Ahriman, glared at Katia and grabbed his arm possessively, indicating that he belonged to her. She displayed her talons as a warning for Katia to keep away from him.

Inside the house, the atmosphere was sombre. Asamara stood in the centre of the room with his hands folded behind his back.

Katia spoke up. "Father, I can explain. We were tricked by the imposters. You know I would never intentionally put the security of the town at risk." Morag cackled, but Asamara walked over to his daughter and struck her face with the back of his hand.

"You foolish girl. I should have used my better judgement and never left you in charge. You have been incompetent," Asamara scolded, while Morag continued to cackle.

"Someone is in trouble. Someone is in trouble." Ahriman turned to Morag. "Silence, you old crone. I am sure Katia tried her best."

Despite her fear of her father, Katia was aware that he also feared Ahriman, who had always had a soft spot for her.

Ahriman took control of the meeting, and Katia watched as her father sat down. It was apparent to her that he had lost weight, his cheekbones and fingerbones seemed more prominent, and he had dark shadows under his eyes. He certainly looked different from the last time she had seen him. In contrast, Ahriman looked muscular, and his blue eyes somehow softened him. He had black hair that reached down to his waist. It was extremely easy to be taken in by his charm and charisma.

"I believe your father is being too harsh on you. You have captured some prisoners, including two powerful elementals. To me, this is good news, and you made the best out of a tough situation. I am not so sure we need to keep the rest of the prisoners. What do you plan to do with them?"

Katia had instructed the guards to keep watch on Carmel when she heard the carriages approaching.

"Bring me Carmel," Katia ordered.

While she waited for the guards to return, she explained her plans for the remaining prisoners to Ahriman and the others in the meeting. "One of the prisoners here is Bartholomew. I am awaiting the return of his twin brother, Bernard. I will ask for his opinion on what he believes is a just punishment. Bernard is a loyal employee of mine, and I do not want to anger him by punishing his brother without his consent. I also have an ex-member of the Black Pioneers with them. I think I will make him my horse, as he was the fastest of the Black Pioneers." Ahriman appeared impressed with Katia's plans so far.

"What do you wish to do with the rest of them?"

"Fang is a shapeshifting wolf who was part of a loyal pack that I have residing here with me; his female companion is here amongst them. I am certain if I reunite them, he will return to her. He has been a lone wolf for too long; he is destined by nature to return to his mate and pack." Ahriman looked to Asamara, who showed no admiration towards his daughter's thoughts or plans.

"It's impressive how you've considered dealing with these imposters. Your father, although a man of few emotions, should be proud," Ahriman complimented Katia. Asamara looked at his daughter and gave a slight nod of approval.

"There is an older man with them called Jo; there is little to be told about him. I think the Valley of the Lost Souls is the best place to send him. He is of no use to me. I have already blocked the elementals from using their powers until I can use them for my gain. However, there is one whom I am worried about. We have Queen Jamillia here, and I perceive she could be a threat to us."

Ahriman considered Katia's honest evaluation. "Do tell. Why do you consider her to be a danger?"

"It is because I have her partner here already, King Jamari. He has become one of my best allies, and I fear if he became aware she is here as a captive, he will abscond and cause a mutiny. There is one more thing to add: one escaped, Ravena, she may have returned to the Underworld to notify them that we have their members as captives."

Vidatu looked incredibly happy with the situation. "Looks like I am going to be able to collect plenty of souls during this battle. It has been a while since I benefitted from multiple deaths. Bring on the battle," he said, with a sinister grin. The guard returned with a terrified Carmel.

"This is Carmel. We were just setting off to the demon town when you turned up."

As Katia finished, her father stood up and addressed her. "I will take Carmel to the demon town. It has been a long time since I spoke to their leader. We were good friends many years ago, and it is about time our rift ended. That will leave you, Katia, in control. I underestimated you."

It was the closest Katia was ever going to get to an apology from her father. She knew that something deep inside of him had changed.

21

It was agreed Asamara would go to the demon town with Carmel. Jahi had been thinking about what they should do with Queen Jamillia.

"I think we should keep the Queen captive and avoid the King from going near that area. As for the rest of your captives, you can use the Queen as a bargaining tool. If they do not comply with your demands, tell them you will kill her; that way, you win and get to stay in control."

The three-headed creature, Dazi Haka clapped in excitement at the plan.

"We like that, yes we do, 'tis a good plan," the threesome chanted.

Ahriman walked up to Jahi and kissed her on her bright red lips. "That is what I love about you - your sharp mind to accompany your deadly talons." Katia felt a pang of jealousy, which Jahi noticed immediately. Before Katia could react, Jahi flew at her, her nails striking out. Ahriman intervened just in time to prevent Jahi from landing a blow.

"Please, ladies, do not fight over me. It would only amuse me. Jahi, using your talons to immobilise Katia would be a danger to all of us. We need her to work with us, not against us."

The town was full of people, animals, and hybrids training to fight and prepare for an attack. Katia felt they had the upper hand fighting on their territory.

They did not know when the attack would happen, but they would be ready. She wanted to test Amber and Kyle's powers out and how they would respond to her command. She summoned for them to be brought from the pit, and instructed the guards to banish Jo to the Valley of the Lost Souls.

The guards arrived in the town square with Amber and Kyle.

"You two, let's have a bit of fun with those powers of yours. Only on a small scale. I want to keep you both strong and not drain your energy just yet." Katia pressed the temples of her head, closed her eyes, and focused her telepathic command on Amber.

"Make the ground shake," Katia demanded.

Amber stood and closed her eyes, focusing on making the ground beneath her feet shake. The ground shook and rumbled as she used her power.

"That is enough. Kyle, your turn now. Make the wind blow the trees."

Kyle extended his arms out in front of him as if he was pushing a heavy object, whilst blowing from his mouth. As he did, a strong wind appeared, swaying the trees backwards and forwards; the leaves from the trees started blowing in the air.

"Stop, Kyle. We do not want a full-blown storm just yet. I am reassured that you can, and both will work to my command. I have decided you and Amber will stay at my home with me. I need you fit and strong. You will be fed the finest foods and cared for in comfort to keep your energies to a full capacity."

***

Back at the pit, the guards were lowering the rope.

"You, old man, climb out." Jo looked at the rest of the group and shrugged his shoulders, not knowing what the guards wanted with him.

"We have been instructed to let you go. You must come with us." The group in the pit looked just as confused.

Queen Jamillia shouted up to the guards, "Where are you taking him?"

The guards showed no emotion as one of them replied abruptly, "It's not your place to be told where he is going. Most of you will be released at some point."

Jo walked in silence with the two guards. He had no arrow set with him, and no way of defending himself. They led him out of town the same way he had entered, and he began to think he might be being released.

"*Perhaps the Underworld has negotiated with the Forbidden Underworld to free me*", he thought. However, when they approached the dense fog, the guards stopped.

"Here is where we leave you," one of the guards said. "Katia has instructed us to leave you in the Valley of the Lost Souls. We will wait here until you have vanished into the fog, and then we know we have completed our job. Katia had no need for you."

Jo felt relieved that Katia still did not know who he was. If she had discovered his identity, she might have held him hostage to lure Ellie to her. However, he was not looking forward to being lost in the fog with all the other souls.

The guards made their way back to the town, unaware of the raven circling over the top of the fog, waiting for them to disappear. Jo was tired and hungry, and he wanted to give up, but then he heard a voice. He thought it was the lost souls starting to torment him with their whisperings.

"Jo, over here." The voice was muffled by the dense fog.

"Who is it? I can't see a thing. What do you want from me?" Jo felt scared and vulnerable.

"Jo, don't panic. It's me, Ravena. I am above the fog and can help you get out. Follow the sound of my voice. The Underworld is preparing a rescue mission, and they sent me back to report. It's a good thing I did, or you may have been lost forever. I saw you with the guards and waited in the tree until it was safe to speak."

Ravena flew above the fog, and Jo followed her voice to stay focused until he could get to safety.

"Not long now, Jo."

Up ahead, the fog was thinning, and Jo could see a gravel path surfacing underneath his feet. Ravena swooped down to the ground and reverted to her human form.

"Grab my hand." Ravena pulled him out of the fog.

"Thank you. I am so grateful. I thought I would never see a familiar face again. Are you coming back with me?" Jo asked. Ravena shook her head in response.

"I need to get back to Katia's town so I can keep watch and report back to the Underworld with any new updates. Are you sure you will be alright if I leave you here? If you go quietly back through the caves, you will be safe." Ravena walked Jo to the entrance of the caves.

"I should be fine, Ravena. Thank you for your help. You need to return to the town and check on the safety of the others. Take care, and farewell."

***

Carmel and Asamara arrived at the demon town during the daytime. It was tranquil, with just the occasional stray dog wandering the streets. The town appeared neat and tidy, much like any middle-class village in the Upperworld. Demons worked hard at night and slept during the day. Their main trade was the illegal market, where they would meet well-known gangsters from the Upperworld and conduct deals with them.

They walked into the town unnoticed. There was no need for security as no one with any sense would dare to attack a demon town. And if they were foolish enough to try, their families would be tracked down and killed. All a demon had to do was catch your gaze for long enough and will you to death with their mind.

There was an odd exception in the demon community that walked around in the daytime, and they were known as day walkers. They emerged, curious about the visitors. Whispering among themselves, one of them recognised Asamara.

"It's him. The master has returned, and he brings with him a young woman. Why are they here?" he whispered cautiously, as he did not want Asamara to hear him.

"Lemuda town is in trouble. I think they are about to involve us in their battle," replied the other youngster.

He was a frequent visitor to the Lemuda town and had been dating a girl from there. Many like him were also visiting Lemuda and dating the demons. The mixing between the younger generations had been growing in numbers.

In the past, a feud developed in the demon town between its leaders. Stories were told of a falling out among the elders that involved Asamara and the present leader. The current leader, Vince Vagorio had been engaged to marry one of the local demon girls, and it was believed he was very much in love with her. At the time, Asamara had been the town leader and took the view that everything in the town was his. He had been very handsome in his youth and combined with his power and riches, was the most influential and eligible bachelor in the town.

Asamara had employed Vince Vagorio's fiancée as his cook, and he would often spend time in the kitchen talking to her. He was taken by her beauty and desired her for himself. When she turned him down, he flew into a blind rage and refused to accept her rejection.

Even though there was an understanding in the demon community never to use hypnotic powers on another demon to lure them for any reason, Asamara didn't care for such rules. Asamara didn't like that he couldn't get his way. He waited until Rose, the young demon girl, was alone in the kitchen, and he used his powers to make her his.

Rose had been under the illusion that she was in love with Asamara, and slowly forgot the love she had shared with Vince Vagorio. Eventually, she forgot Vince altogether. Knowing his wrongdoing, Asamara took her and some of his loyal followers to the new town, Lemuda, and the Forbidden Underworld was created.

***

The shadowy figure of Asamara walked up to Vince's door and knocked. The door opened, and for the first time in years, the two adversaries faced each other.

"How dare you show your face here? Get your hand off my door and leave now."

As soon as he opened the door to Asamara, anger rose inside him. The shock of seeing him resurfaced emotions as if it had been yesterday for Vince. He had tried to move on in his life, but he had never settled or forgiven Asamara.

"Please, Vince. I do not come seeking forgiveness; I have come to ask for your help. I have brought someone with me whom I need you to listen to. If you do not wish to speak to me, then at least hear her out."

The house in which Vince lived had once belonged to Asamara. Nothing had changed since he had left; even the furniture remained the same.

"Please have a seat," Vince said as he turned to the young woman. "What is your name?"

"Carmel," she replied, feeling anxious about her request.

"We need your help in Lemuda town. The Underworld is preparing for battle and will come with both force and excellent fighters. The feud between you and Asamara is irrelevant to the younger demon communities; it is seen as ancient history. They want to be able to roam freely between the two towns and meet their lovers without hindrance. They will not stand back and watch Lemuda being attacked, risking the loss of loved ones and friends. For the sake of our towns, you must put an end to this now."

Vince squirmed at the fact that he could not refuse her demands. In their community, it was a tradition to help other blood demons, and Carmel held this as her bargaining tool, despite having been forced by Katia to do her bidding.

"Then I will grant your wish. I will talk to my people and tell them the importance to help in the pending battle. It is clear they need to be aware of the danger facing their loved ones." Vince's loyalty lay with his people and not Asamara.

"Please return soon, Carmel. You have a home here anytime you may wish to return."

"Thanks," Carmel replied, even though she knew it may not be possible for her to ever return.

Carmel had no choice but to go with Asamara, back to the Forbidden Underworld. While they had been in the demon town, Katia had taken it upon herself to release Fang, Jasper, and Bartholomew from the pit but kept them under her command to not utter a word to anyone that Queen Jamillia was being held captive. The threat to kill the Queen had been enough for them to keep quiet. Several members of the demon community had already started to turn up for the battle, vowing to help the Forbidden Underworld from destruction.

22

Jo had arrived safely at the heavy metal door separating the two Underworlds. Since he had no key, he used the rusty doorbell to signal to the Underworld that someone needed entry. Members of the Grand Council went on high alert when the doorbell rang, but Bob Bomtane's quick thinking soon reassured everyone.

"This must be someone we know; Katia would never announce an attack. I will go; everyone else is busy," said Bob.

He scurried down the tunnel, grunting with each step, and soon arrived at the door.

"Who is it?"

The familiar voice of Jo replied, "Bob, it's Jo. I am by myself and have not been followed."

Bob slid the keys under the door as he was not tall enough to reach the lock. As the door opened, it revealed Jo's stressed face.

"Welcome back, Jo. How did you escape?" Bob asked as they walked back to the Underworld. Jo explained the turn of events and Ravena's goodwill.

"Bob, I need to go find a woman named Shareena. She's a psychic who can help me find Beth. I've been told that she's not dead. Please don't tell Ellie just yet that her mother might be alive." Bob looked shocked by the revelations.

"I agree. It's best not to tell Ellie until further

information is obtained. Take care on your journey. We don't know who our enemies are at this time."

***

Both sides were now prepared as best as they could be and had assembled their armies in the fleeting time they had. It was not the battle they wanted, but the Underworld had no choice; they needed their friends back, and the Forbidden Underworld knew they were coming for them. Miss Beadle, the Underworld secretary, sat at her desk with an old typewriter, compiling an inventory of the number of fighters and weapons that would be used in the battle.

INVENTORY.

Thirty defender monks with staff and spade (each)

One hundred army bees with a sting

Ellie, elemental fire

Octavian, elemental water

Ten shapeshifting fighting panthers with striking claw skill

Twelve shape-shifting white stallions with a hind leg drop

Five shapeshifting tigers from the Jamari clan with predator skill

Eight whirlers with whirling combat

Eric and Erna, the two fighting polar bears with the ability to punch through twenty inches of ice, lethal to any other living thing.

This was the best army of invaders the Underworld could gather at such short notice, but it was a good one. The army had been told to assemble at the recreation area at five o'clock so they could be counted and check that their weapons were in good working order.

Grandpa Jo managed to find Ellie to say goodbye before she set off into battle. Ellie ran into Grandpa Jo's arms.

"You're back. Are you hurt and are the others with you?" Ellie was speaking fast, and Grandpa Jo was struggling to keep up with her.

"Ellie, I'm not hurt, but I had to escape. Unfortunately, the others are still there. It's been quite an ordeal, and I'm feeling exhausted and emotional." Grandpa Jo met Ellie's concerned gaze.

"What about you, Ellie? This will not be easy, and you must stay strong and remember everything you have learnt. I don't like goodbyes, so I will say it now." Ellie hugged her grandpa as if it were the last time she was going to see him, and then turned away crying to head back home.

***

Members of the Forbidden Underworld had assembled in the town square and were doing a headcount of all their fighters. Gino was tasked with recording the number of fighters present.

Fifty Div
Fifty Deem

Thirteen Black Pioneers, including Jasper, with deathly trample

Thirty demons with brain-crushing telepathy, including Carmel, Ahriman and Asamara

Amber elemental

Kyle elemental

Pack of shapeshifting wolves 15 strong, including Fang. Deadly bite.

Katia and Jahi with hypnotising eyes, immobilising fingernails, telepathic blocking and controlling powers.

Morag the Hag with deception, illusion, and a vast array of spells

Dazi Haka with fire-breathing flames

Vidatu with poisonous green vapour emanating from his mouth, deadly to humans, collector of souls

Bartholomew under Katia's control. Strength of six men. Bouncing rolling attack. Speeds of up to 60 miles per hour

Rawcus, the wrestling bear with the ability to crush if he gets hold of you. Never lost one out of the 2000 fights he had.

Both sides had deadly fighting teams, and it was impossible to say who would be the stronger side.

***

Back in the Underworld, the fighters gathered.

"Welcome, all you brave warriors. This is the last time we will speak for a while. As you are aware, some of you may not make it back," Bob said solemnly.

He directed his last sentence to the bees, as this was a life-or-death battle for them. They were prepared to die, and using their sting would be fatal for both the bee and the victim.

Bob held a large ceremonial horn and blowing it would start the beginning of the battle.

"Good luck, and bring our friends back," Bob said.

The horn sounded, and the warriors set off to the toboggan pods, ready for their descent into the Forbidden Underworld. The army of bees would be flying through the catacombs and following the toboggans.

***

Jo arrived back at Pear Tree Farm and knew he had battles and demons to overcome. With Bill still helping at the Underworld, Jo had the privacy to do an online search to find Shareena. After a quick search, he found a Shareena located in his village, just as the woman in the Valley of Lost Souls had told him. The online advertisement read: '*Mystic and Psychic. I will tell you what is hidden from you. No time wasters. Please call to make an appointment.*' Jo inputted the number into his phone. The phone rang, and a female voice answered.

"Hello, Shareena the mystic and psychic. How can I help you?"

Jo hesitated nervously before speaking. "I'd like to make an appointment with you for a reading."

"Ah, yes. Is this Jo? I've been waiting for you to call. I can give you an appointment for tomorrow at 10 in the morning, if that's acceptable for you," Shareena replied.

Jo was taken by surprise that she knew his name. "How did you know my name?" Jo asked.

Shareena laughed. "It's my job to know. I have been waiting for you for a long time. It's best not to talk over the phone, you can never be sure of who is listening." Jo confirmed the appointment would be fine.

"I live at 65 Rochester Terrace, by the side of the post office in Billingham village. I bid you farewell, until tomorrow." Jo knew it would be a long night, with the worry about the battle and the anticipation of news of his daughter's whereabouts.

23

The fighters raced to the Boggopods and strapped themselves in. They descended towards the Forbidden Underworld at high speeds, twisting and turning rapidly around the catacomb bends. One by one, the toboggans began to stop, and the fighters got out to assemble into their respective fighting groups. Meanwhile, the army of bees buzzed loudly into the catacombs, hovering, and waiting to enter the passage leading to the Forbidden Underworld.

The passage was pitch dark, and the end was not visible to the human eye. The walls were rotting, emanating a pungent smell of dampness. The monks were adept at using their senses, so they did not need any light. They walked steadily, without fear. The monk leading the group suddenly stopped and held his hand in the air, signalling that danger lay ahead. They held their staff and spade in a defensive position, ready to fight anything that might come their way.

The Div and the Deem were spotted ahead, snarling with saliva dripping from their jaws in the shadows. The foul smell of decay emanated from their breath.

"Prepare to honour the Underworld," the master monk shouted, and the battle began.

A large Deem charged at four monks, but they quickly blocked it using their staffs as a barrier. The monks jumped into the air simultaneously, wielding their staffs, and ran over the top of the Div and Deem, effectively trapping them from both sides.

At the other end of the passage, a group of monks stood in perfect silence, chopping through the air with their hands. Three Deem came charging towards them, but the monks, in one graceful movement, leapt up and extended their legs straight out, kicking the creatures and sending them flying into the air. The Deem crashed down to the ground with a sickening thud, landing on the four smaller Div and leaving them injured.

The monks ceased wielding their staffs and stood with their backs against the wall of the passage, staring at the entrance. After witnessing the monk's superb display of skills, Ellie stood motionless with them. Suddenly, the wind started to build up in the passage, and a moving, blurry object was seen passing through quickly, knocking everything over in one swift motion, as if it had made a perfect strike in bowling. It was one of the Whirlers.

A loud humming sound could be heard as a swarm of bees flew in with their steel stingers. They administered their stings with precision, enough to stun and injure the Div and the Deem without endangering themselves. This would leave the creatures sedated for several hours, giving the warrior fighters enough time to exit.

They made their way up the passage to another door with limited security; it was as if it had been made easy for them to pass through.

"Here we go. We don't know what we'll be facing, but so far, no one has died. Let's try to keep it that way. We'll probably get separated, so if that happens, return here," Octavian ordered.

Upon opening the door, they found themselves in the town square, which was deceptively quiet and deserted.

"This is not good," Ellie remarked. "They could be hiding anywhere."

No sooner had she spoken when a loud siren sounded in the town, alerting the residents to the arrival of the attackers. Katia rode out on one of the Black Pioneers and circled them, laughing uncontrollably.

"Do you think you can defeat us with your small, pathetic army? Leave now before you are destroyed."

Ellie looked around as the residents emerged from their hiding places; she was undeterred by Katia's threats.

"We have just defeated your creatures in the passage, do not underestimate us," Ellie replied.

Katia laughed even louder. "I still have plenty for you to defeat before you even get anywhere near your precious friends."

The warriors were surrounded by the fighters of the Forbidden Underworld and were outnumbered.

One of the monks whispered to the group, "Remember: fear is a state of mind, and death is only temporary. Control your breathing, stay focused, and don't forget, our mission is to get our friends back safely to the Underworld."

Thirteen Black Pioneers moved forward and stood apart from the rest of the fighters. This signalled the white stallions to move forward, ready for combat. The two herds of horses walked up to each other and met in the middle of the town square. Jasper had no choice; he feared that if he did not fight for Katia, then Queen Jamillia would be killed.

As the horses engaged in headlocks, there was a lot of head shunting. One of the Black Pioneers reared on its hind legs and lunged forward with such force that it nearly knocked over one of the white stallions. Both herds were now in full battle, using their hooves to cause maximum injury.

Several horses from both sides were injured and exhausted by the ferocity of the fight. Cheers could be heard coming from the residents of the Forbidden Underworld.

"Go, Black Pioneers."

It was common for them to watch fighting for their entertainment.

"How could anyone want to watch this for fun?" Ellie exclaimed in horror.

She recognised Jasper by the white central stripe running through his mane; he was a fierce and strong fighter. Jasper had the upper hand, and the white stallion went crashing to the ground, its white mane stained with blood.

Jasper was about to bring his forelegs down on the already injured horse, likely killing it. Its eyes were wide, and its nostrils flared as it let out an awful screeching noise. However, Jasper slammed his legs down within an inch of the stallion's head and could not bring himself to kill it.

Jasper hung his head in shame and tucked his tail in a submissive position. He knew he would have to deal with the consequences of Katia's beatings later. As a result of the severe injuries on both sides, some being near-fatal, the competing herds stopped fighting; neither side had the energy to continue.

Rawcus, the wrestling brown bear, was angered by the Black Pioneers' defeat and Jasper's refusal to kill. He stepped into the middle of the town square and roared at the top of his capacity, swiping the air with his sharp claws to beckon the two polar bears into what was to become his wrestling arena. Ellie shook with fear and was too scared to watch the fight.

Rawcus ran at Erna, swiping his claws at him. Erna charged headfirst back at him, but it did not hinder the bear as he wrestled him down to the ground. Rawcus stood up, roared, and body-slammed Erna, winding him in the process.

Eric, after seeing his injured brother, ran at Rawcus, catching him off guard. He punched Rawcus with full force in the face, sending him reeling to the ground. What happened next was a shock to everyone.

Rawcus sat down with his head bowed and refused to acknowledge Eric. He showed defeat with a submissive stance, indicating that he no longer wished to fight. Eric retreated from the bear, never turning his back on him in case he was bluffing. Rawcus could not defeat Eric due to his level of aggression, fuelled by seeing his injured brother.

Ellie watched in amazement as the once-undefeated bear now admitted defeat. Eric also wanted the fight to end so he could attend to his wounded brother. The Forbidden Underworld crowd showed no compassion, with shouts and jeers.

"Boo! Get up and fight, coward!" the crowd jeered at Rawcus.

He hit the ground in front of him and stared at the crowd, giving them a warning to back off. It worked, and they went silent. Ellie felt a sense of sympathy for the bear, who seemed to have no choice but to fight in the Forbidden Underworld.

The wolves didn't hesitate to take their turn to fight, their hunger for blood apparent after watching the previous battles. Fang remained at the back of the pack, showing great reluctance to fight or attack. Meanwhile, the panthers from the Underworld began to prowl slowly. Two of them climbed a nearby tree to observe the events while the rest of the panthers stood their ground in silence. The wolf pack circled them, snarling and baring their fangs.

The wolves were about to attack when three of the panthers swiftly moved first, pouncing on their victims. The first wolf went down, whimpering as the panther held it by the throat, stifling the wolf's ability to breathe. The second wolf received an almighty slap from a panther's heavy paw, sending it flying into the air. One of the wolves had been bitten badly by the panther and lay bleeding on the ground. The rest of the wolves did not get a chance to attack before the two panthers in the trees jumped down in silence and landed on two of the wolves, biting their backs and immobilising them.

Four of the wolves had managed to corner one of the panthers. One of the wolves ran at the panther and bit its nose, while another wolf attacked its throat. The wolves then backed off, leaving the panther to die. Ellie couldn't take it anymore and ran into the midst of the fighting animals, screaming.

"Stop, Katia. It's me you want. Face me now and fight me here," Ellie demanded.

Katia clapped, emphatically.

"I will not fight you, but I have two people who are a match for you and Octavian."

The animals in the town square, still hungry for blood, backed off at Katia's command. Octavian stepped forward to stand with Ellie. The pair stood back-to-back, scanning the area, ready to defend themselves against any attack.

"Are you ready for this?" Octavian checked.

Ellie stood her ground. "Yes, I am, without a shadow of a doubt."

From the crowd, Amber and Kyle stepped forward, under the control of Katia to face Ellie and Octavian; a blank expression adorned their faces. Amber focused her energy, causing the ground to shake violently beneath them, while Kyle raised his hands, summoning the clouds. The clouds began to swirl, and an almighty gust of wind arose. Ellie and Octavian clung to each other with all their might.

"It's our turn now. I know you two don't mean to do this."

Octavian breathed in and out rapidly, and hailstones the size of golf balls began to pelt the town members, knocking several of them out. Ellie extended her fingers and pointed to the sky, summoning lightning that struck the ground all around them. All kinds of demons and creatures ran, shrieking and falling to the ground, burning.

The monks stood in a line and chanted a mantra.

Octavian shouted to Ellie, "What are they doing?"

Ellie was not sure, but Kyle managed to speak up. "It's an ancient unblocking spell. They are unblocking the spell Katia has placed on us," Kyle explained.

A handful of demons approached the monks, each choosing one to stand in front of and hypnotise. The demons were preparing to use their powers to crush the monks' brains. Carmel, however, ran behind the monks for safety and stood, staring back at the demons. She had decided to break the code of her kind and help the monks.

The demons' gaze had no effect, as the monks' chanting and Carmel's powers combined to protect them. The chi energy they created repelled the demons, causing them to hold their heads and writhe in pain. Several of the demons fell to their knees, holding their heads in agony. One by one, they began to combust, leaving nothing but fragments of dust particles floating in the air.

Katia screeched at Dazi Haka, "Get in there and kill the monks!"

The three-headed, fire-breathing creature jumped into the battleground and started breathing flames at the monks. Despite being surrounded by flames, the monks continued to chant.

Octavian shouted to the sky, "Unleash your power."

Torrential rain hit the ground and extinguished the flames. The flames turned blue and shrouded the monks, covering them in ice, but their chanting was still heard. Dazi turned to Ellie and breathed fire straight at her. Ellie held her hands in front of her and repelled the fire straight back at Dazi. She spun around and pointed her finger at Dazi, striking the creature with a fireball that hit one of its heads directly. The head screamed in agonising pain. The creature ran at Ellie and was within seconds of reaching her when it was sent flying into the air, as Bartholomew picked it up and threw it.

Katia signalled to the rest of the Div and Deem to join the fight. "Go kill them or pay the price yourselves," she shouted.

The army of the Div and Deem ran forward, grunting as they went. Three of them ran towards Bartholomew, but they were no match for his strength. Bartholomew picked up two of them and smashed them together in the air while kicking the other one out of the way. Kyle battled two more of the beasts; he summoned his wind energy and blew them backwards with tremendous speed. Amber ran to the tigers and the remaining uninjured panthers.

"Hurry, we must go. Queen Jamillia is still held captive in the pit. She is surrounded by Div and Deem and can't get out. King Jamari must be informed of her whereabouts," urged Amber.

King Jamari had been one of the spectators of the battle and was too stunned to do anything other than watch. The panthers and tigers split into two groups: one to get the King and the other to rescue the Queen.

Ellie was amid a fierce battle with Dazi Haka when the creature breathed out a fatal blast of fire at her. Although she was consumed by flames, Ellie felt no pain. In response, she ran towards the creature, leapt through the air, and landed on it, causing the two of them to become a blazing fireball. Amidst the chaos, Dazi Haka's three heads could be heard screaming in agony.

By the time the remaining elementals realised Ellie's danger, it was too late to do anything about it. Kyle tried to summon the wind to blow out the flames. The town itself had gone deadly silent as everyone watched the bodies engulfed in flames. There was a force field around the two of them, stopping the other elemental's powers from working. The flames had now turned white with the intensity of the heat, and Ellie and Dazi fell to the ground, not moving.

As the flames engulfed them, Ellie could be seen separating from Dazi, his severely burnt body lying on the ground, lifeless. Ellie had defeated Ahriman's most fearsome fighting creature.

Kyle shouted to Octavian, "Ellie is going to die. Help her, do something."

Kyle dropped to his knees, sobbing uncontrollably; the wind was still blowing from the storm he had created. It blew the ashes into the air around them. The ashes began to form together and developed into the shape of a creature; it was a phoenix.

The wingspan of the phoenix was 15 feet long, and as it glided into the sky, it shone gold. Breathing fire out of its mouth, it swooped down to the ground next to Kyle and Octavian. The phoenix shook its feathers and transformed back into the familiar form of Ellie.

With a smile, Ellie spoke up. "You didn't think I would leave you now, did you?"

The warriors of the Underworld cheered in celebration and ran to hug her. Kyle and Amber were visibly relieved that Ellie had survived the ordeal. Octavian had taught her an important lesson about immortality, and now she had emerged victorious.

Octavian looked relieved as he addressed her, "You managed to resurrect into the phoenix. However, be warned that another immortal can take your life. Enemies will come, and they will undoubtedly try to uncover this knowledge on how to kill you. Worse still, if someone does discover this information and, heaven forbid, kills you, they will absorb your power and become even stronger. The identities of the Keeper of the Keys, who are the only ones who know how to kill you, are hidden." Ellie wasn't fully processing the information as she was still grappling with her transformation.

The warriors surveyed the carnage in the town square, but there was no sign of Katia and her gruesome supporters. They had gone into hiding for the time being. In the distance, Amber's voice could be heard shouting.

"Over here. Come and help us."

Amber was standing on a hill in the distance, frantically waving at them. The fighters were about to leave and assist Amber when a fast-moving large object rolled into Bartholomew, knocking him over.

Once everyone had a chance to focus on it, they saw it was on top of him. It was not attacking him; it was hugging him. The object, now human, spoke.

"Did you think I would fight you, my brother, my twin? Blood is thicker than water. That's something Katia and her clan don't understand," Bernard said as he helped his brother up.

"It's good to see you, Bernard. What about your wife and child? Are they safe?" Bartholomew asked with concern.

Bernard let out a sigh. "Oh yes, I sent my lovely Tamara and newborn, Brodie to our clan in Scotland. No one dares mess with the Mackenzie clan. Too many of them have our strength, including the women. They are in safe hands." Bartholomew laughed in agreement.

"So does the Underworld need another pair of fighting hands? I am here to offer my services and to stand by you."

Octavian looked at Bernard's hands and nodded. "I think I speak for the rest of the group with a yes; those hands are more like shovels." Everybody laughed.

Bernard turned to the monks. "What's with the chanting frozen monks? Is someone going to help them?"

Ellie had forgotten about the frozen monks. She walked over to them and placed her hands on the ice block that surrounded them. The heat and energy from her hands melted the ice to reveal the monks chanting. Their eyes returned to normal, and they looked relieved that the battle had stopped, for now.

24

The warrior group set off up the hill to where Amber was standing in the presence of a pacing angry King Jamari. Halfway up the hill, they spotted a lone figure. Ellie stopped in her tracks, her face pale and distressed.

"Ellie, what's wrong? You look like you've seen a ghost," asked Kyle.

Ellie pointed at the woman on the hill. "I have. It's my mum. I don't understand, how can this be?"

The woman on the hill smiled at her with her arms held out in a welcoming manner. "Ellie, my sweet darling, don't be scared. It is me, your mum. I never died on 'that day'. I have waited so long to see you, but Katia kept me captive. During the battle, someone let the prisoners out, and I was one of them."

Ellie ran towards her mum, exhausted and crying. She was about to reach her mum's arms when she noticed she had turned into a hag. The hag was Morag, using her spell of illusion and deception to capture Ellie.

Morag the Hag cackled. "We will get you Ellie and kill you, just like Katia and the wolves killed your mother." Ellie flung herself forward to strike Morag, but Octavian grabbed her.

"Ellie, stop, she is not worth it. This trickster will get her karma in due course, of that, I am sure." The persistent cackle from Morag grated in Ellie's ears. Morag in true style vanished in a haze of mist.

Amber ran down to Ellie to console her. Tears dripped down her face as she sobbed uncontrollably.

"Ellie, we will all be at your side for as long as we can. You don't have to do this by yourself," Amber reassured her, holding onto Ellie tightly.

***

The monks had not spoken since being broken free from the ice. Bartholomew noticed they were acting strangely, staring into the distance, and had stopped chanting. He enquired if they were alright.

"Our demon shadows are coming to fight us," exclaimed the monk.

They banged their staffs on the ground, and shadows appeared in front of each of them. The fight began, and with every move the monks made, their shadows replicated it with even greater strength. These shadow monks were the dark side of the monks. According to their history, the moment they started fighting, their battle was already lost.

The monks were trained to protect, not kill, but by killing the demons, they knew that their souls would be taken. Despite this knowledge, the monks performed their best moves, but with each strike, the shadow fighters increased their ferocity. For their final move, the monks ran in the air as if running up a wall and extended their right legs to deliver a powerful kick to the shadow fighters. The shadow fighters replicated the move, and one by one, the monks fell to the ground, their demon shadow selves merging back into their lifeless bodies.

Ellie felt a chill run down her spine as Vidatu appeared before her. He had come to claim the recently deceased souls of the fallen monks. She watched in horror as Vidatu inhaled and absorbed their souls, imprisoning them within his own body for all eternity. His smile gave her the creeps as the green vaporous residue of the consumed monks escaped from his mouth.

Ellie's heart pounded as she heard panicked voices shouting. She knew something was wrong as her eyes searched for danger.

"Run! We have Queen Jamillia! Run back to the passage!" Octavian's voice cut through the chaos, urging the group to flee and prepare the toboggans.

"Kyle and Ellie, stay with me. We must ensure the King and Queen return with us safely."

Amber stopped and abruptly shouted urgently to the sky, "Universal spirit, hear my cry, crumble this hill."

Ellie felt in grave danger as she realised the fighters from the Forbidden Underworld had emerged at the top of the hill. Ellie thought there was no hope, but the ground began to rumble and quake beneath their feet. She watched in awe as Amber joined forces with them as they held each other's hands and chanted.

"Universal spirit of air, fire, water, and earth, hear our cries. We are your vessels, use us and destroy this land," their voices filled with urgency.

Ellie could feel the power of their words as they vibrated through her. The group stood together, united in their purpose, and at this moment she knew that they were capable of anything.

Ellie's heart thumped loudly in her chest as the dark sky lit up. She watched in disbelief as the town's residents were struck by lightning, causing their bodies to be flung down the hill by an electrical force. Then, with a deafening roar, the wind tore up the hill, knocking everything over in its path, and torrential rain washed away everything in its way. Ellie knew these were the forces of nature they had summoned together with their elemental powers.

A deafening sound ricocheted through the air and the ground split open and formed a massive crack down the centre of the hill, mud pouring down the slope. But the worst was yet to come. Although these were their enemies, Ellie watched in horror as people were lifted in the air and dragged towards a twisting tornado that had formed on the hill. The vortex sucked in the town residents and creatures as it whirled past them.

The tornado raged down the hill, sweeping people with it and dropping them through the crack in the earth. Ellie could hear their screams ringing in her ears as they were swallowed up by the mud and debris. As the mud cascaded down the hill, it filled the crack in the earth and the people and creatures within were lost forever. Ellie felt tears streaming down her face, but she knew they had to keep fighting. If they stood together, there would be hope.

The elementals had completed their mission of destruction on the residents of Lemuda town. They turned their backs on the hill and walked towards the safety of the toboggans, ready to reunite with their loved ones and share their victory. Despite the excitement, Ellie couldn't ignore the heavy weight of sorrow she felt for those who had lost their lives. As she looked around, she noticed Fang, who appeared injured and concerned.

"Some of the toboggans are missing. I have counted them, and they're gone. The track is also warm, indicating recent use," Fang informed them as he limped over. In his human form, he knelt and sniffed the ground.

"I suggest someone has used them to head towards the Underworld. Evil has been here. We must hurry. I smell danger," he added.

Without hesitation, Ellie and her fellow warriors strapped themselves into the toboggans, pressed the buttons, and jetted off back through the catacombs. A sense of dread filled Ellie's mind as she thought about what awaited them.

The Boggopods came to a stop and Ellie felt a sense of relief wash over her. The still-healthy warriors assisted the injured out of the toboggans, but the eerie silence that surrounded them was not what she had anticipated, and there was no celebratory welcome awaiting them.

As they made their way to the Grand Council meeting, Ellie couldn't ignore the uneasy feeling in her stomach. As she approached the meeting room, she heard groans and whimpering, causing her to hesitate before opening the door.

The sight that greeted Ellie could only be described as a nightmare, and she recoiled from the scene. Injured people and animals were strewn across the hall, their faces etched with pain. Sighs of relief flooded the room as the injured realised their companions had returned. Bob urgently outlined the situation.

"They came here, Jahi, Ahriman, and Asamara. They told us you were all dead. Jahi used her nails to kill and maim people and animals. The luckier ones are in the sick bay for 24 hours, until the immobilising poison wears off. Ellie, I'm afraid your dad is one of them," Bob explained urgently.

Ellie paced up and down, overwhelmed by the news. "This explains why we didn't see all of them at the battle; they deceived us. I will kill her. She killed my mum and now her bullies are trying to kill my dad. I will destroy them." Ellie's rage grew.

"This next part, I'm afraid, will only increase your anger. They captured Ravena on their way here and tortured her in front of your dad to extract information from him." Bob looked uneasy as he recounted all the details of the events, but he had to bring Ellie up to speed.

"Your dad believed Katia had killed you, so he told them he was your father and Beth's husband, and that he would stop at nothing to avenge your deaths. Unfortunately, his efforts could not save Ravena. Jahi killed her in front of your dad and even took Ravena's feathers to add to her coat as a trophy."

Ellie's vision blurred as tears fell from her eyes. A mixture of grief and relief washed over her. Ravena was gone, but at least she had not lost her dad.

"Your dad tried to stop her, but she struck out at him, scratching his face and immobilising him. She thought she had killed him, as your dad's heart temporarily stopped beating. Lady Marabelle has given him one of her life-saving herbal tinctures, so he is safe."

Ellie's knees buckled, and she crumpled to the ground, overwhelmed by the devastating news.

"Oh God, where is Grandpa Jo?" Ellie stammered, fear making it difficult to take in any more negative news.

"No one knows, Ellie. All we know is that he was not here when the attack took place. Another worrying issue is that Asamara took the map of the land where the Keepers of the Keys reside. We had been entrusted with this map to keep it safe, and now it has been taken from us." Ellie's face paled; she knew all too well the importance of the Keepers of the Keys.

"This means that if you ever resurrect into your highest form as an immortal phoenix and Katia finds the hidden knowledge, she can and will use it to kill you. So, if you don't transform, this knowledge will be useless."

Ellie's shoulders slumped, and she let out a heavy sigh. "I'm afraid it's too late, Bob. I have already fully transformed. I had no choice; it was the only way to save my life and everyone else's." Bob's snout whiskers twitched nervously.

Ellie turned to Amber, her voice trembling as she spoke. "Can you come with me to the sick room? I'm too anxious to go alone." Amber nodded, and the pair made their way to the room.

Ellie approached her dad and gently took his hand. She leaned in close and spoke in a soft voice, barely above a whisper.

"Dad, it's me, Ellie. I have returned safely. I would never leave you alone to suffer." She paused, her eyes full of tears, before continuing. "But I have to go and find Grandpa Jo. He is missing, and I know you would want me to find him."

Ellie felt her dad squeeze her hand in acknowledgement of her words.

"I will return tomorrow and hope you will be better. I love you." She gazed at him, searching for another sign that he had heard her.

Ellie's heart pounded as she left the Underworld to go and find Grandpa Jo. She glanced back at the old oak tree. To any passer-by, it would have appeared to be just a standard tree. However, Ellie knew of the destruction and carnage that had just occurred beneath the ground. As she walked, she spotted a beautiful young woman in the distance with a basket in her hands, collecting items from the ground. Ellie watched, captivated as the young woman ate what she had gathered.

The woman's humming and singing intrigued Ellie, and she watched with envy as she happily wandered through the woods. For a fleeting moment, she wished she could have changed places with the woman, just to have a sense of normalcy. As Ellie continued on her way, the woman was soon gone from her mind. Her focus returned to Grandpa Jo, and her pace quickened as she ran back to Pear Tree Farm. She hoped Grandpa Jo would be there, unharmed and resting peacefully.

As Ellie hurried on to find Grandpa Jo, she never heard the words to the woman's song.

"I am young again with the youth of a girl. I have work to do in the Upperworld. I am young again with the youth of a girl." Ellie had not realised the woman was Morag the Hag.

Whilst everyone had been preoccupied with the final attack on the Forbidden Underworld, Morag had seized the opportunity to go and collect magic acorns. The Fae usually guarded these acorns to stop the likes of Morag from getting her greedy hands on them. Despite the acorns being known to be poisonous to ordinary folk, Morag had eaten them already, and true to their powers, they had restored her youth. She now resembled a beautiful young woman, and there was no telling what damage she could cause to the people in the Upperworld. There would be plenty of people to manipulate and deceive.

25

As Jo walked towards the village, his mind was solely focused on reaching 65 Rochester Terrace, located next to the post office in the village. He had no clue whatsoever about what had happened in the Forbidden Underworld or the Underworld.

Within 15 minutes, Jo arrived at the house. It was a pleasant-looking terraced house with a vibrant red door and gold numbers displaying the number 65. The house was surrounded by a small array of colourful hanging baskets and garden statues, which made the small, paved terrace bright and cheerful. Ornamental butterflies adorned the walls, and a wooden chime swayed in the gentle breeze, creating a delicate, melodic sound.

Jo felt nervous as he knocked on the door and waited for an answer. He could hear the security chain being removed from inside the house and the door slowly opening. As the door opened, Shareena greeted him.

"Hello, Jo. Nice to meet you, my lovely," she said as she held out her hand toward him. "Do come in."

As he entered, the narrow hall was filled with the scent of incense sticks. Jo observed Shareena as she welcomed him. She appeared pleasant to the eye, in her 40s, dressed casually in jeans and a jumper. Her unruly hair had strands of grey in it, and her eyes showed a depth of wisdom gained from the experiences she had in life. Shareena reassuringly smiled at him as she took his coat.

"I hope you don't mind dogs. I have one called Blaze. He's my adorable husky and an excellent security dog. One can never be too cautious these days. In my line of work, you never know who may turn up for a reading." A black and white husky walked in and stood by her side. Jo went to stroke the dog, but it snarled. Shareena explained, gesturing to the husky,

"Blaze can be a bit temperamental with strangers, but he means no harm. At ease, Blaze. Jo will not harm me."

Shareena calmed the dog down with a gentle pat. Jo followed her to a small, but pleasant room at the back of the house. The room was filled with multiple books arranged neatly on shelves. Crystals of all shapes and sizes were dotted about the room, catching the light, and giving it a mystical feel. Several pictures of fairies lined the walls, adding to the enchanting atmosphere of the room.

Shareena guided Jo to a table with two chairs. He sat down, taking in his surroundings and was fascinated by the mystical objects and books surrounding him.

"Would you like a drink before we start?" Shareena asked.

Jo politely declined, eager to find out what she had to say. He noticed that the table was covered with a purple velvet cloth, and on top of it lay a red satin pouch. Jo watched curiously as Shareena opened the pouch and removed a blue, unpolished stone and a pack of cards.

"This is my Lapis Lazuli, imported from Egypt. I use it as a seer stone to help me with my psychic readings," she explained, holding the stone up for him to see.

Shareena then bowed her head and proceeded to say a spiritual prayer, calling upon the divine loving spirits to guide the reading.

"Divine loving spirits, help me provide Jo with the truth and the initiative to understand what he needs to do. Blessed be." Jo felt a sense of calm wash over him as he listened to her words.

Shareena smiled and handed Jo the 78-card tarot deck.

"Please shuffle the cards, and with your mind, heart, and spirit, ask them your intentions. Be clear about what you want, and we will gain more clarity from the cards." Jo shuffled the cards and focused.

"I ask you to keep your intention in your mind."

"*Please tell me the truth about my daughter, Beth. Is she still alive?*" Jo thought to himself.

Shareena sat with her eyes closed in a meditative state as he observed her. She opened her eyes as he stopped shuffling the cards.

"Are you happy with your question?"

Jo nodded enthusiastically. "Yes."

"Good. I need you to spread the cards on the table face down, hover your hands above them, pick ten cards, and pass them to me. Please use your left hand to choose the cards as it is closest to your heart. You will feel a warm, pulsing sensation in your hand; this will tell you the correct card to choose."

Jo closed his eyes and concentrated on his question about his daughter, Beth. As he passed his left hand over the cards, he felt a warm tingling and knew which cards to choose. He picked his ten cards and passed them to Shareena.

Shareena held the Lapis Lazuli stone in her hand and placed the cards face-up, arranging them in a Celtic cross. As Shareena spoke, Jo listened intently, trying to absorb her words.

"Jo, you have new beginnings ahead. A battle has needed to happen to get these beginnings. Although the battle has taken place, do not become complacent as there are many battles to still fight. The cards are showing me a new building and meeting place. They are also giving you courage and strength," Shareena said. As she spoke of courage, Jo felt a surge of determination inside himself.

"The cards show me that you have lost someone close to you, and you will find this person again in the coming months. The card does show death concerning this loved one, but this is often not the case. The death card represents new beginnings and rebirth." The mention of the death card made Jo feel uneasy. As he reflected on Shareena's words, he felt a mix of emotions: hope, fear, determination, and uncertainty.

"Shareena, does this mean my daughter is alive?" Jo asked desperately.

Shareena gently placed her hand on his shoulder.

"Jo, I can see your sorrow and I don't want to give you false hope. However, it feels like your daughter is still in this earthly realm and not the spirit realm." Jo clutched his hands to his chest in anguish, wondering if it could be true that his daughter was still alive.

"Let me see if the cards can offer you more clarity," she said as she reached for the deck and reshuffled them. "They show a journey that you need to go on. This is a long journey, to the top of a mountain with a path running up it. You will need to conquer the demons and creatures that lurk along the treacherous path."

"If this is what it takes to find my daughter then I will embark on this journey. Do you see anything else, please Shareena?" Jo asked, his voice quivering with emotion.

"I see that you will face many challenges along the way. The moon on this card indicates that there will be many illusions to deceive you. In these situations, you must choose the correct path to take. The cards are showing me the Devil." Jo's heart raced at the ominous cards.

"The Devil will bring unscrupulous people into your life but don't be worried, Jo. Remember, you have been dealt the Courage card to help deal with whatever is thrown in your path."

"This is a lot to take in and I hope some good can come from this." He studied the cards laid out on the table, trying to make sense of their meanings.

"Jo, at times it may feel like all hope has gone from your life, but please do not give up. Hope is on your side. The reading shows a bright shining star guiding you. When the Star card appears, it brings wish fulfilment into your life."

Jo wiped a tear from his eyes. He knew he had to face unscrupulous people on his journey. Despite the challenges ahead, Shareena's words of encouragement gave him hope.

"I know your question is still not answered as clearly as you may want. So, please, my lovely, allow me to consult my crystal ball."

"I'm happy with the predictions and how you have interpreted them. I've never paid interest in mysticism before. If I'm honest, I would have called it mumbo jumbo, but not after today. My eyes have been opened," Jo said. He watched as Shareena moved the tarot cards to one side and reached for a large crystal ball.

"Jo, hold this in your hands and focus your mind on your question again. Before I begin the crystal ball reading, do you have a photo of your daughter? It will help me if I can visualise her," Shareena explained.

"I keep a picture of Beth with me; I also have her locket." Jo reached into his pocket and gave the locket to Shareena.

"Brilliant, Jo, an item of jewellery and a photo. I can use psychometry and my seer stone to conclude your reading and then give you the answer to your question." Jo handed over the photo and looked on with curiosity.

As Shareena held the locket in her hand, she closed her eyes and took a deep breath. After a few moments, she opened her eyes and looked directly at Jo.

"I see a large volume of dark, murky water. A woman is sinking deeper and deeper into the water, drowning, but then something saves her. It doesn't seem possible, but it's what I see." Jo looked concerned as he waited for Shareena to continue.

"Jo, this is the lady in your picture. Did she have an accident in the water? I need some confirmation before I continue with the reading as it is showing me something strange. I can't make sense of this."

Jo replied, "Yes, my precious daughter drowned, but her body was never retrieved from the quarry lake."

Jo observed Shareena, who looked worried about the images she was being shown.

"As a psychic, I am aware of the dangers of opening oneself up to spiritual attacks. This is unlike any reading I've done before, and I am concerned about the entities we may be dealing with."

"Please, Shareena, continue. You have been amazing so far, so don't doubt what you see, no matter how obscure it may be." Jo was relieved and grateful.

Shareena took a deep breath to continue. "Wait, there is more. I can see another woman with two wolves looking down into the lake. They saw your daughter resurface. I cannot make sense of this. The two wolves are now women. They jump in the water and drag her out; it is them that save her. They tie her hands behind her back and take her somewhere. A lady dressed in purple appears to be giving the instructions."

Jo's heartbeat pounded as he listened. His face was fatigued and drained of colour, but he was also elated that his Beth was alive, as he trusted Shareena's words.

Shareena brought the crystal ball over her right shoulder as she explained the process.

"I am retrieving the information," she said.

The crystal ball clouded over inside as Shareena examined it intently. As she began to speak, the voice was not hers; it was Beth's.

"Dad, it's me. Please come find me. Katia has taken me somewhere. I am on a very high mountain entombed in ice. I can hear, breathe, think, talk, and see everything around me. The mountain folk that reside here think I am their saviour, and that the evil ones cannot be defeated until I am freed by those who love me."

Jo wiped the sweat from his brow, feeling a mix of relief and worry.

"Of course, I will come and find you, nothing can stop me."

Jo was interrupted further by Beth's anxious voice. "The villagers have tried in vain to free me but to no avail. The Dark Lords know where I am. They reside in the witches' lair and are protected by all manner of spells. Find the Dark Lords, and you will find me. Come quickly."

Jo felt a wave of terror wash over him. He couldn't imagine what kind of danger his daughter could be in, but he knew he had to do all he could to find her.

Shareena slumped forward on the table, and Jo rushed to her side, worried about her well-being. She moaned and lifted her head.

"Oh, my lovely. I hate it when I go into a trance," Shareena said, her voice weak. "Beth must have a strong presence. This happens when an old incarnate possesses my body." Jo watched as Shareena stumbled to the kitchen and returned with a couple of mugs of herbal tea.

"Drink this, Jo. It will calm your nerves. It's an infused ginseng tea and an added guarana spell enchantment to replace our lost energy. It is draining to go through a big reading like today, so we need some replenishment." Jo was appreciative of the brew.

"Who is Ellie? She was calling your name and looking for you, when I was doing the crystal ball reading, she looked distraught," Shareena added.

"She is my granddaughter." Jo looked panic-stricken.

"You better go to her. May I ask a favour? A place called the Underworld came through to me during the reading, and I would very much like to help. Please could you take me there sometime?"

Jo nodded; he couldn't refuse her after all she had done for him today. "Of course, I will, as soon as I can, and once I know Ellie is safe. I'm sure the Underworld would be grateful for your help and your gifts. Thank you so much for your time and energy, Shareena. How much do I owe you for the reading?"

Shareena shook her head. "Nothing, my lovely. This one is on the house. Some things in life you cannot put a price on, and this is one of those occasions. Thank you for coming to me for help."

With a sense of gratitude, Jo left Shareena's house and headed home, eager to see Ellie and start unravelling the mystery of Beth's disappearance.

26

Ellie's heart leapt as she heard the door open. She knew instantly that it was Grandpa Jo. She hurried down the stairs to meet him.

"Ellie, you're safe!"

Ellie rushed into his arms. "Grandpa Jo, I'm here, I'm fine," she reassured him, though her anxiety was still etched on her face.

"I have so much to tell you. Dad has been hurt. Don't worry, he is being taken care of. Many of our people and animals have been injured. The Underworld is no longer safe, and we need to find new accommodation."

As Jo paced around the kitchen, Ellie became concerned about why he was on edge.

"I too have some news. I think we need to sit down and have a cup of strong tea while I tell you."

Ellie made two cups of tea and sat down next to him at the table. Both looked tense and worried. As he took her hand, Grandpa Jo spoke softly.

"There is no right way to tell you this news, Ellie." She braced herself for the worse. "You must understand what I am about to tell you is the truth. I have been told this news on three separate occasions. Your mum, my Beth, is still alive. She is lost, and we need to find her," Grandpa Jo said.

Ellie felt a jolt of shock and disbelief as Grandpa Jo's words sank in. *Could it be true? Could her mum still be alive*? She held her cup so tightly that her knuckles turned white, trying to process the news.

"Are you sure this is true?" Ellie asked, her voice trembling. "How do we find her? Where do we even start?"

Jo squeezed her hand gently. "This has been an issue troubling me in my mind, but I now do not doubt that this is the truth. We'll find her and do everything we can to bring her back to us."

Tears welled up in Ellie's eyes as she looked at her Grandpa Jo. *Could they find her mum after all this time*? She was willing to do whatever it took to bring her mum back home.

"What do we need to do, Grandpa? How do we find her?" she asked, her voice full of determination.

Grandpa Jo took a deep breath and began to explain. He told Ellie about the witches, Dark Lords, and how they knew where her mum was hidden. He spoke about the mountains where her mum remained frozen in time. Ellie listened intently.

"We still have a long way to go before we find your mum. I'm afraid it won't be easy, and no doubt more people will be at risk of losing their lives. We need to go and address the Grand Council and Bob Bomtane and ask for advice. The prophecy states that it must be love that can release her from the ice. Others have tried and failed, but they have no love connection to her."

"I'll do whatever it takes," she vowed, her voice firm.

"I know you will, Ellie. You have your mother's strength and determination. We'll find her together," Grandpa Jo said with a smile, his eyes filled with love and admiration.

"It's going to be a dark and dangerous journey, especially when Katia finds out. She will send her minions to try and stop us. Your mum had many hidden depths and gifts that she chose not to explore. She never wanted to draw attention to herself or her family. If Katia had known about her power, she would have tried to obtain it."

Ellie was aware that while Katia and her followers were currently focused on their journey to find the Keepers of Keys and their secret knowledge, they would eventually turn their attention back to her and seek to eliminate her.

"I transformed into the phoenix, and even though I am immortal, Katia can kill me if she gains the keepers' knowledge," she explained.

Ellie knew that this news would be a burden for her Grandpa Jo.

"I wish there was a way to put an end to Katia's evil. Wherever she goes, she causes pain and destruction, all in the name of power and control. There must be a way to defeat her?" Ellie asked.

***

As Rose reminisced about her past, she thought about how she had met Asamara. When he arrived in her town, it was poor and in desperate need of wealth. He had told Rose that he inherited wealth from his late father and that he would use it to build his empire in the town, thereby also increasing its prosperity. Rose had fallen under his spell and had fallen in love with him, and hadn't been aware of his deceptive use of power to make her his.

Rose had not been subjected to Asamara's barbaric cruelty until the birth of their first child, Katia. During the difficult birth, Asamara had refused to be present, considering it beneath him, as childbirth was a task for women only. His only concern was whether the child was male, as he desired a son to be his future heir and to train in his evil ways. When he learned that Rose had given birth to a girl, he flew into a blind rage. Although Rose had contemplated leaving him, she feared for her life at the time, so she stayed.

As the years went by, Asamara spent less and less time with Rose and Katia, focusing instead on building his empire. Rose felt trapped in a loveless relationship and sensed Asamara's impatience for a son and heir. She eventually agreed to have another child.

Rose quickly became pregnant, and as the pregnancy progressed, she sensed the child was different. One night, she had a dream that the child she was carrying was a boy and that his blood held magical powers.

Rose consulted with her midwife, who told her of an ancient prophecy of a child whose blood could stop the demon bloodline from becoming evil and corrupt. However, there was a catch: if the demon's heart became too dark, the child's blood could cause death. Rose knew that Katia's heart had already turned dark, influenced by her father's evil ways.

This caused a dilemma for Rose because she knew one drop of her unborn child's blood could cause Katia's demise and the rest of the evil demons would dissipate too. Rose struggled with what to do, torn between her love for her daughter and the greater good of stopping the corrupt demon bloodline.

Rose was convinced that her unborn son was the one prophesised to carry the powerful blood. As much as she loved her daughter, she was devastated by the fact that Katia had chosen to follow her father's evil ways. If the prophecy was true, her unborn son would either save her daughter or cause her death.

When her child was born, Rose knew what she had to do. She pleaded with her midwife to help her escape with the baby, even though it meant leaving her daughter behind. It was a painful sacrifice, but Rose believed it was necessary. She knew that although Asamara would still care for Katia, he wouldn't bother to pressure her about her doing his evil bidding as she was not a male.

Rose knew that Asamara wouldn't want to be present during the birth of their child, so she devised a plan with the midwife. The midwife agreed to tell Asamara that his son had died during childbirth and that Rose had left him because she couldn't face him after the loss. It was a painful deception, but Rose felt it was necessary given the details of the prophecy.

Upon hearing that his child had died, Asamara went into a blind rage. The midwife was terrified that he would discover the truth and punish her, so she kept quiet about the escape and never spoke of it to anyone again. Rose knew she had to keep her son hidden and safe, even if it meant leaving her old life and the people she loved. She prayed that her sacrifice would be worth it.

After leaving Lemuda, Rose found refuge with a family of demons living in the caves. They welcomed her and her newborn son, Kyle, and helped them until Rose was strong enough to continue her journey. The demon family never asked about Rose's past or the identity of the child; they simply wanted to help a young mother in need.

They made sure that Rose and her new baby were prepared for their journey to the Underworld. Emilia, the demon lady made a baby blanket for Kyle with the initials K.P. The P stood for Perithington, Kyle's father's surname. Emilia never knew what the initial stood for. Rose kept the truth about Kyle's father buried deep in her heart to protect her son.

Rose couldn't help but feel a sense of regret for leaving her daughter behind. She knew Katia was loyal to her father. Rose had not anticipated that Katia would challenge her father's views on her ability to rule his kingdom due to her gender.

There were signs of Katia's soul growing darker as she tried to gain her dad's affection, in the hope she could become heir to his kingdom.

As Rose journeyed towards the Underworld, she wondered what kind of future lay ahead for her children. *Would Kyle truly be the one to stop the demon bloodline from becoming corrupt? And what about Katia? Would she be able to resist her father's evil ways and forge her path in life?* Only time would tell.

Rose left the demon dwellings and set off through the remaining caves. Feeling exhausted and weak from her journey, she knew she had to keep going. Clutching Kyle to her chest, she stumbled through the winding caves, but despite the danger that lurked around every corner, nobody dared approach her. It was a universal understanding that a travelling mother with a newborn child was to be left alone and unharmed.

After what felt like an eternity, Rose managed to find her way to the entrance of the Underworld. She mustered up the last bit of her energy and ran towards the door, calling out for help. The tiny, strange-looking creature known as Oggle Boggle had sought solitude in the dark corridor when it heard her cries.

As Rose collapsed at the door, Oggle Boggle sprang into action and went to get help. The Grand Council welcomed Rose and her newborn child, offering them a safe place to stay. However, despite their kind offer, the following day Rose took the difficult decision to leave Kyle behind and slip away.

Rose was determined to never let Kyle question her about his father. She kept this information buried deep in her heart to protect him from the truth. However, Rose's involvement with the Underworld was soon to change, either by chance or fate.

***

As Ellie and Grandpa Jo returned to the Underworld after a good night's sleep, they were both wiser about the recent events that had taken place in their lives. The usually bustling Underworld was now eerily quiet, and security had been tightened. Ellie observed Bartholomew and Bernard pacing around the corridors, both carrying walkie-talkies to report anything suspicious.

They headed straight to the sick room to see her dad. As they approached, Ellie's heart sank as she worried about his condition. She and Grandpa Jo stood outside the sick room, discussing when to reveal the truth about Beth still being alive.

"It's too soon to tell him about Beth. I think the shock would be too much until he recovers," said Grandpa Jo.

"I agree. We can tell him in a few days," replied Ellie.

As they entered the room, Bill's eyes twitched, as if he could sense their presence in the room. He called out to her.

"Come and give your injured dad a big hug and kiss. I'm so glad you're safe, Ellie. I feared I had lost you too, and I couldn't bear it if I did." Ellie felt the anxiety leave her body, and she hugged her dad, who grimaced with pain.

"Go easy on the hug. I'm still not out of the woods yet and still in a lot of pain. The poison in my body will take time to leave before full recovery."

Grandpa Jo wiped a tear from his eye as he hugged Bill.

"I'm so relieved, Bill. You need to get on the mend as soon as possible. We still have a lot to do. Ellie and I will go and find Bob and update the Grand Council with the news we have."

Ellie looked at him and gave him a gentle smile, to show her appreciation for not mentioning the need to request a team of volunteers for the upcoming mission to find her mum.

Ellie and Grandpa Jo entered the Grand Council meeting room where they found Bob in his usual place. Volunteers were busy cleaning the room after the devastation.

"Hello, you two. Grab a broom. There's plenty of work to do. The classrooms still need cleaning."

Ellie began to explain what Grandpa Jo had told her. Bob agreed that they needed help and did not insist on their participation in the cleaning.

"This is a matter of great urgency, and you will need an excellent team to go with you. The challenges you will encounter will be the most dangerous you have faced to date. I will contact Blue; he has been tracking in diverse places in the Upperworld, so Lady Marabelle will need to use her usual communication skills to find him."

"We need to wait until my dad gets better. We haven't told him yet; we fear he is not strong enough with the poison still in his system. Too much shock will cause his body to go into overdrive," Ellie explained to Bob.

He let out a deep sigh, indicating his understanding of the situation.

"Yes, your poor dad feels like it's his fault Ravena died. I can imagine he is feeling very fragile." '

Ellie scanned the room and asked, "Where are Kyle and Amber?"

"I sent Kyle and Amber to the Upperworld. We need a new building, so they are looking for new premises for us all to relocate to," Bob revealed.

Ellie was taken aback by this news. "Why the Upperworld? How are the animals going to join us at our meetings?"

Bob seemed to have anticipated her question and was ready with an answer.

"I'm afraid we have to move. Katia and her followers could return at any time, and they know we have been weakened." Bob handed her a brochure and she scanned the description.

"Abbington Hall, that sounds perfect," she said, admiring the photos from the large estate. "But how will we afford it?"

Bob sighed. "We'll have to dip into our emergency funds, but it's worth it to keep us all safe." Ellie nodded in agreement and handed the brochure back to Bob.

Ellie had known of the old hall since she was a child. It had been magnificent in its day, but now it was shabby and in need of love and attention.

"What do you think? Do you like our potential new premises? I'm sure we can all give it the attention it needs to be restored. It comes with a large greenhouse and an old barn."

"I love it, Bob. I don't mind helping with the restoration, but I won't have much free time with our mission to find my mum."

"Don't worry, Ellie. I know you would help if you could. There is an exciting factor in Abbington Hall; it has an old wine cellar with three large rooms and a door linking to the catacombs. It will be easy to transfer the toboggans there," Bob explained.

Ellie's face softened at the idea of a new, safer location for their meetings, it made her feel more secure.

***

While standing outside Abbington Hall, Kyle and Amber awaited the arrival of the estate agent. Despite being fashionably late, he eventually pulled up in a flashy red sports car, causing Kyle to roll his eyes in annoyance.

The estate agent introduced himself with a smug look.

"Hello, it's good to meet you. David Appleby is the name and selling is my game." Kyle found the man's arrogance irritating.

Appleby was dressed in an expensive black pinstriped suit, with his brown hair gelled back. Even his fingernails had been manicured.

"If you don't mind me asking, aren't you two a bit young to be buying a property of this size?" David Appleby asked, looking the pair up and down. "I do hope you're not wasting my time. This property is on the market just short of a million pounds. Judging by the way you are both dressed, you don't look like you can afford it. How would you be expecting to pay?"

Kyle felt his blood boil at the estate agent's condescending tone and resisted the urge to lash out, and instead opened his rucksack to reveal the considerable sum of money they had brought with them.

Amber scowled at the estate agent's response. "You really should not judge people. We will be paying cash and the full asking price, so you don't need to worry about us wasting your time. The way I see it, you are wasting our time. And don't worry, you'll get your commission," Amber chimed in, laughing at the estate agent's embarrassment.

David Appleby stammered. "S-sorry, but you have not even seen the hall yet. It requires repairs. If we go to the main entrance, I believe the housekeeper will show you around the property," he said, addressing Kyle.

As Kyle and Amber approached the door, the estate agent followed closely behind. A woman in her 40s greeted them and introduced herself as the housekeeper.

"Hello, is this the 11 o'clock appointment, Mr Appleby?" the housekeeper asked, looking up at the estate agent but not visually focusing on the faces of Kyle and Amber.

"Yes, it is, Miss Newton. I think it would be best if you showed these two around," Mr Appleby said, his shoulders slumping as he muttered to himself. He then headed back to the car to wait for confirmation of the sale after the viewing.

Kyle could tell that the estate agent was annoyed with him, but he didn't care. The housekeeper greeted them with a smile.

"Come with me, I will show you around the property. I know it so well, having lived here for years. Can I ask for your names, please? I have a big house to show you, and I don't want to be rude by not knowing your names," she said.

Amber gave the housekeeper a warm smile. "I am Amber, and this is Kyle."

The housekeeper stopped in her tracks and looked at the young man, seeming taken aback by him. Kyle felt uncomfortable under her gaze and grimaced.

"I'm sorry, I did not mean to stare, I'm Rose. You remind me of someone from my past," Rose stated.

When the owner died, they had stipulated in their will that the new owners would keep on the faithful housekeeper. The Grand Council was aware of this requirement when they looked at potentially buying the hall. Rose gave the couple a curious look.

"How come a young couple like you two are buying a property so big? I hope you don't mind me asking?"

Kyle decided to answer honestly, knowing that the housekeeper would eventually learn the truth from the Grand Council. He knew there was no point in lying to her. He also knew that the Council had been discussing ways to remove Rose from the property by offering her a large amount of money and new lodgings, but she had refused vehemently.

Kyle began to explain to Rose. "We are part of an organisation that deals with environmental and animal welfare issues, and we need a new base; our old offices are not big enough." Kyle wondered if the housekeeper had any idea who their organisation was.

"The house is impressive from the outside," Kyle commented, hoping that the interior would be just as appealing.

Abbington Hall was just as impressive inside as it was outside, with its shiny wooden floors and moulded plaster on the ceilings. Large chandeliers filled the rooms, and wooden beams added to the warm atmosphere of the hall. Several rooms were adorned with large stone fireplaces. The kitchen was generously sized, and although it had modern features, it still retained many of its original fixtures.

Kyle and Amber followed Rose upstairs to the sleeping quarters. Amber's excitement was contagious, as she let out a loud squeal when she saw the bedrooms. Without hesitation, she ran into one of the rooms and jumped onto the large wooden four-poster bed, giggling with delight. Kyle couldn't help but smile at her joy.

"This room is mine. I love it. It's all old and spooky. I bet ghosts are haunting here," Amber exclaimed with excitement. Kyle watched as Rose smiled at Amber's enthusiasm, as she turned to him.

"What do you think of the hall, Kyle?" Rose asked, curious to hear his thoughts.

"It has potential," Kyle responded stoically, not revealing his true feelings about the hall. "Please, can we see the wine cellars?" he asked.

"Of course, you can." Rose led the pair downstairs to a white-painted wooden door next to the kitchen.

"Mind your heads on the way down, the ceilings are low."

Once down in the cellars, Kyle had to stoop. He quickly spotted the door that led to the catacombs.

As Kyle looked at the door, Rose warned him, "You see that door? There is a legend the door leads to underground caves, but I would not recommend going down there without an expert; you may end up getting lost."

Kyle again wondered if Rose knew anything about the Underworld and looked at her suspiciously. He asked, "Do you have the key for the door?"

Rose patted the side of her hip where a large bunch of keys swung on her belt and replied, "Yes, I have the master key for all the doors. I will be honest; that particular door has not been opened since I've lived here."

With that, Kyle and Amber's tour of Abbington Hall was complete. Rose scanned their faces for a response.

"Do you think you will be purchasing the house on behalf of your organisation?"

"Yes, we will. It is perfect for all our needs," Kyle said confidently.

Rose smiled warmly at the pair. "This is excellent news, I'm glad to hear it," she said. "I will bid you both farewell for now, and I am over the moon that I will be your new housekeeper." Amber and Kyle said their goodbyes.

As they approached the estate agent's car, Kyle noticed that Appleby seemed preoccupied with his appearance in the car mirror. He tapped on the window, startling Mr Appleby.

"We will be purchasing Abbington Hall today," Kyle announced.

Appleby snapped out of his self-absorption, his face breaking into a wide grin. "Good. I gather you like the property? Jump in, I will take you back to the office, and you can sign the papers." Kyle and Amber climbed into Mr Appleby's car, eager to finalise the purchase of Abbington Hall.

As they drove off, Rose watched them with a heavy heart. She knew what she had to do: contact the Grand Council and reveal her identity. It was the only way she could stay at Abbington Hall, and yet, the thought of exposing her secrets made her uneasy. She took a deep breath and reminded herself that it was the right thing to do. Rose would have to face the consequences of her past actions, but it was time for her to finally confront her demons.

Rose reached for the small carved box sitting on her dresser and retrieved the key from the chain around her neck. With a trembling hand, she unlocked the box, revealing the phone number for the Underworld inside. Bob Bomtane had given her the number years ago, in case of emergencies.

Rose took a deep breath, her hands trembling as she dialled the number, her heart racing with anxiety as the phone rang. A gruff male voice answered.

"Underworld. Bob speaking. Who is calling, please?"

Rose paused for a moment, gathering her thoughts before speaking. "Is that Bob Bomtane?" she asked.

"Yes, it is. Who is speaking?" Bob responded.

"Bob, it's Rose. Kyle's mother and soon-to-be your new housekeeper at Abbington Hall."

"Goodness me, Rose, we wondered where you had gone."

"I met Kyle with young Amber, but I did not tell him who I was. I had a feeling you would try to get rid of me as the housekeeper, but I am asking you to keep me on. I feel you are all in some danger, and I want to be near my son and help the Underworld." Bob held the phone tightly in his hand as he listened with intent.

"How do I know we can trust you," Bob asked.

Rose could hear the suspicion in his voice. She took a deep breath before answering.

"I understand your concern, but you have my word. I am willing to do whatever it takes to prove my loyalty to the Underworld and to protect my son. I have nowhere else to go, please let me stay," she pleaded, hoping her words would be enough to convince him.

Bob remained silent for a few moments before responding.

"Alright, Rose. We will keep you on as housekeeper."

She breathed a sigh of relief before continuing, "There is one last thing. Kyle's father is Asamara, and his sister is Katia."

Bob sighed heavily on the other end of the phone. "Rose, this is a most dangerous situation. We are at war with the Forbidden Underworld, and your daughter will stop at nothing to kill us. I am not sure telling this news to Kyle is a good idea."

"I understand the danger, Bob. I will tell him myself if I have to. I am saddened that my beautiful baby Katia has turned to her father's evil ways. But if she is a threat, Bob, then we need to be prepared. As much as it pains me, I need to explain to Kyle that there is a way he can stop her from continuing down this path of darkness." Bob listened quietly, his mind racing with the implications of what Rose was revealing.

"One drop of Kyle's blood mixed with Katia's can destroy or save her," Rose revealed.

The thought of Kyle having to confront and potentially harm his sister was almost unbearable, but they had no other option. They were at war and needed to do whatever it take to survive.

"Rose, this is terrible. Are you saying Kyle has the power to stop this evil?" Bob asked, his voice filled with concern.

"Yes, we are in much deeper than you could ever have imagined. Bob, will you tell the Grand Council everything?" Rose asked, her voice filled with anxiety.

"For now, Rose, it's best to keep the information about Kyle and Katia quiet until I know what to do next," Bob replied. Rose sensed his unease and sighed. "I understand, Bob. I just hope we can find a way to keep Kyle and those residing at Abbington Hall safe from the Forbidden Underworld," she said, her voice determined. As she ended the call, Rose couldn't help but wonder what would happen next.

27

As preparations for their move to a new home were underway, Ellie couldn't help but feel the sense of excitement in the air. Octavian bustled about, giving instructions on what needed to be packed up and loaded onto the toboggans. The toboggans would transport everything to the catacombs beneath Abbington Hall. For many of the Underworld residents, the only home they had ever known was being left behind, and the added stress of the recent battle was taking its toll on everyone.

Ellie watched as Oggle Boggle tried to manoeuvre a pulley truck loaded with boxes.

"Oggle Boggle, be careful with those boxes; they have breakables in them," Octavian ordered.

As Oggle Boggle sang to himself, Ellie couldn't help but smile. He provided her with a welcome distraction from the stress of the move.

"I'm leaving my home, and I'm leaving it all alone."

Ellie listened to Oggle Boggle's little song and felt a pang of sadness. The little creature did not know how to express its feelings conventionally, but its words struck a chord with her.

The estate agent had told the Underworld residents that they could move into Abbington Hall with immediate effect. Ellie felt a sense of relief wash over her, knowing they were leaving the danger behind. The thought of being above ground and away from Katia and the Forbidden Underworld brought a sense of ease.

As they made their way to Abbington Hall, Ellie couldn't help but feel a little disappointed that she wouldn't be able to help with the renovations. But she knew that she had a mission to prepare for and that her skills would be needed for the fight to come.

Today was the day Ellie would tell her dad that her mum was still alive. She took a deep breath as she approached the sick bay area where her dad was recovering. Lady Marabelle had given the all-clear for him to be informed about the new developments while he was still in the sick bay, in case he went into shock.

As she entered the sick bay, Ellie saw her dad propped up on pillows, looking weak but alert. Bob Bomtane was standing by his side, a concerned look etched on his face.

"Hi, Dad," Ellie said, trying to sound cheerful.

"Ellie, my dear. How are you?"

"I'm good, Dad. But we need to talk about something important," Ellie said. "It's Mum. She is still alive."

Bill held his heart, and his expression turned to one of concern. Ellie took a deep breath and continued with everything she had learnt from Grandpa Jo about her mum's survival and the upcoming mission to find her.

Bob interjected with additional details and explanations, making sure he understood the gravity of the situation. Bill was silent for a moment.

"If I am to take this as being the truth, when do we need to set off to find the Dark Lords?"

Ellie leaned forward and wrapped her arms around her dad's shoulders, giving him a tight hug before pulling away to answer the question.

"In two days," she said, her voice steady and determined. "I know it's not much time to prepare. Bob has already started organising everything for us." She took a deep breath before continuing. "We are going with a strong team. Blue will be joining us, and we'll have Octavian, Kyle, and Amber as well. Grandpa Jo will be coming too, and Lady Marabelle, due to her familiarity with the witches at the lair."

"This can't have been easy on your emotions," Bill expressed. Ellie could see the surprise in her dad's eyes.

"It hasn't been easy, but I know what we need to do. On a positive note, we get to stay at Abbington Hall tonight. The Grand Council has arranged a get-together with food and music," Ellie added, her heart lifting at the idea of having some fun and a chance to unwind. She knew it would be a while before she would have another opportunity like this.

Lady Marabelle had conducted Bill's final health check and agreed that he could leave the sick bay. Ellie walked alongside him as they departed.

They were going to their home first so that Bill could shower and collect his belongings before heading to Abbington Hall. For safety reasons, they had all decided to stick together.

***

Rose was familiar with arranging social events at short notice. Back in its heyday, Abbington Hall had been a popular venue for socialites. However, this time was different. Rose wanted it to be a night to remember, and she was looking forward to watching her son enjoy himself with his friends.

Rose couldn't help but feel a twinge of sadness. Her son, Kyle, would soon be leaving on his mission, and she didn't know if he would return. But for now, she pushed those thoughts aside and focused on the task at hand. She watched as the caterers bustled around the kitchen, preparing food to cater for every dietary need. The tantalising aroma of sweet and savoury dishes wafted throughout the hall.

Rose had gone for a festive look, adorning garlands, balloons, and party streamers in every corner. She had made sure to add a touch of whimsy and colour to appeal to the younger members of the Underworld.

The 'Flying Fiddlers' trio had arrived, setting up their instruments and microphones. Rose had heard wonderful things about them; their traditional Irish songs were sure to get everyone on their feet. She stepped back and admired her event planning, proud of the ambience she had created.

***

Ellie sat on the couch in her home with her dad and Grandpa Jo, discussing the possibility of finding her mum alive.

"I can't believe it," Bill said, shaking his head. "After all these years, she could still be out there."

"I know, Dad," Ellie replied, "But we don't have much time to dwell on it. The party at Abbington Hall is starting soon."

Grandpa Jo chimed in, "And we need to be ready for our next mission. Don't forget your backpacks. It'll be a while before we see home again."

Ellie nodded, feeling a sense of both apprehension and enthusiasm about the mission ahead. She looked out of the window and saw Blue pull up in his truck.

"He's here," she said, grabbing her backpack. "Let's go."

"It's good to see you again, Blue. Where on earth did you vanish to? The last time I saw you was at the gates of the Forbidden Underworld, and then you were gone," Jo said.

Blue looked thoughtful for a moment, and Ellie sensed that there was a story behind his disappearance. He took a deep breath before answering Grandpa Jo.

"It's a long story, my friend, involving the Zolontoff people - a great little community in the middle of the Indian Ocean," Blue explained. "They needed help finding one of their clan members. Somehow, they had gotten caught in an undercurrent and drifted off into another dimension, somewhere near the Bermuda Triangle. Tricky one, but I got them back to their people."

Jo nodded in admiration, clearly impressed with Blue's skills.

"Excellent work, Blue. It's such a relief to know we're in good hands, and we appreciate your help."

Ellie watched as Bill carefully piled the bags into the back of the truck. Finally, they were all set to go to Abbington Hall. She could feel the excitement building inside of her as they approached the gated driveway. They had all made an effort to dress nicely for tonight's party. Grandpa Jo had put on his best shirt and trousers and Bill had followed suit.

"We clean up nicely," Ellie said, admiring the small group's appearance.

As for herself, she had opted for her black flares with stars on and her favourite vintage t-shirt, a prized possession that had once belonged to her mum. Bill had tried to persuade her to wear a dress, but Ellie was having none of it.

Blue hit the telecom button, and a familiar voice answered, "Password, please," Bernard requested.

"Pink Elephants," Blue answered. Ellie couldn't help but let out a chuckle.

As the gates opened, she felt a rush of excitement, eager to see what lay beyond. As they drove through, she let out a gasp of amazement. '

"Oh, it looks so pretty all lit up," Ellie said, admiring the scene.

She could see that Rose had outdone herself with the decorations. The whole place was illuminated by beautiful lights, which had been hung up by volunteers from the Underworld. Ellie loved how the solar lanterns lining the path to Abbington Hall looked like dancing flames.

The music was already blaring out of the hall, and Ellie found herself swaying to the beat. The air was filled with laughter and chatter, and she knew her friends were inside somewhere. With a huge smile on her face, Ellie rushed towards the hall, eager to join in on the fun.

Ellie's eyes widened as she stepped into the hall. The soft ambient lighting gave the space a magical feel, and she let out a gasp of awe. Lady Marabelle had furnished the room with faux mushroom tables that looked like they had come straight out of a fairy tale.

The disco lights flashed and bounced off the walls, casting a rainbow of colours across the room. Ellie could feel the energy in the air as people and creatures alike danced to the latest tunes. She scanned the room for her friends and Amber's wave caught her attention.

"Ellie, over here," she called out.

Amber looked fabulous in her black lace skater dress and Converse, her curly hair flowing naturally around her face. The pair made their way to the dance floor. Kyle appeared out of nowhere and poked Ellie in the side, causing her to squeal in surprise.

"Hey, watch it!" she scolded playfully, unable to hide the smile that had crept onto her face. "I see you've made an effort," she teased, taking in his usual attire of jeans, t-shirt, and boots.

"Thanks, Ellie," Kyle said with a grin. "I'll have you know it's a brand-new top." Ellie couldn't help but laugh at his predictable banter.

The music went quiet, and Ellie's attention was drawn to the stage where Bob Bomtane had taken his place.

"Hi, everyone. I would like to welcome you all to our new home and headquarters. We have invited you here tonight to let your hair down; we know there will be more challenging times ahead of us." Ellie felt a twinge of sadness.

"For now," Bob continued, "please give a big round of applause to our guest band for the night, 'The Flying Fiddlers'." The crowd erupted in cheers, as the band made their way onto the stage.

The lights dimmed in the hall, and twinkling lights were projected onto it, creating a starry effect. Aerial silks extended from the ceiling with three people balancing on them with impressive ease, each holding a fiddle. The sound of their fiddles echoed throughout the hall, adding to the already mesmerising performance.

The crowd watched in amazement as the trio moved their bodies in perfect synchronicity. The combination of ethereal lighting, aerial acrobatics, and the beautiful music made for an unforgettable experience.

The trio played fast-paced songs that made the crowd dance and jump around, and then seamlessly transitioned into hauntingly beautiful melodies. The group consisted of two males and one female, with the female taking the lead as the vocalist. Her voice was like that of a siren, and Ellie felt the hairs on her arms stand up in response.

As the performance drew to a close, the Flying Fiddlers descended from the aerial silks to face the thunderous applause from the crowd. However, the show was far from over. With a burst of energy, the trio leapt off their silks and performed multiple backflips while still playing their fiddles. Ellie cheered and wrapped her arms around her friend, grateful for the incredible experience.

"I've loved tonight. I've danced so much my feet hurt," Amber chuckled in response.

"Did you see Kyle stomping around? He even tried Irish dancing!" The two friends burst into laughter, embracing each other once again.

Kyle joined in on the fun, despite his lack of skill on the dance floor, he was having the time of his life.

"That was amazing!" he exclaimed. "No wonder they're called the 'Flying Fiddlers'!" The musical trio met their fans and signed autographs. Ellie had felt blissfully distracted, until her attention was drawn to her dad, Grandpa Jo, Blue, and Lady Marabelle sitting together at a nearby table. While the party had raged on around them, they had huddled together, deep in conversation.

"Goodness me, you lot. Did you not join in with the dancing and fun?" Ellie asked.

"My dancing days are over, Ellie."

She rolled her eyes at her dad's reply, not accepting his excuse. "Give over, Dad. You're not an old man yet. Grandpa Jo, you should've danced with me."

"Sadly, we have had so much planning to do, in such a short space of time. I am glad you have enjoyed the evening; it is what you should be doing at your age."

Grandpa Jo's words made Ellie pause for a moment. She could see the worry in his eyes. She wanted to tell him everything would be okay, but she knew it wouldn't be.

Her dad looked her in the eye. "We are all worried about the future. We are not going to lie to you. We have had a heated debate on whether the young elementals should even come on the next mission." Ellie was about to object, but her dad interjected.

"Don't worry, we decided we couldn't do this mission without you all. You are the ones with the power." Ellie knew in her heart her dad's words were the truth, after all, they were the 'Elementals'.

ABOUT THE AUTHOR

S.L. Saunders grew up in the northwest of England and has been lucky enough to enjoy the rural countryside, which has had a profound influence on her writing. She is passionate about educating others on preserving the beautiful natural aspects of the planet we call home.

The adventures of Ellie and the Underworld have been in the making for the last three decades, originating as a story told to her two children at the time (now three). Previously a teacher in further education, her circumstances now allow her to dedicate more time to her lifelong passion for writing, which began in her early childhood.

Pictures from her youth often depict her surrounded by books and sitting with her typewriter, painting a picture of her true ambition in life. Combined with her love for animals and the environment, it becomes clear how Ellie and the Underworld sprang to life in Sharon's imagination.

ACKNOWLEDGEMENTS

A big thank you to my daughter for designing the artwork for the book cover. Also, thank you to my editor and publisher, Green Cat Books, for their kind words of reassurance when I needed them. I would also like to express my gratitude to my family and loved ones for their patience, understanding, and words of encouragement.

For more information about our books or publishing services, please visit
www.green-cat.shop